Café Dulcet

A Novel by
Chiquis Barrón

www.chiquisbarron.com

This is a work of fiction. Names, characters, places, and
incidents either are the product of the author's
imagination or are used fictitiously. Any resemblance to
actual events, locales, organizations, or persons, living
or dead, is entirely coincidental and beyond the intent
of the author or publisher.

Books by Chiquis Barrón may be purchased for educational, business, or sales promotional use. For information, please write: Chiquis Barrón, P.O. Box 254, Cortaro, AZ 85652-0254 or visit www.chiquisbarron.com.

SECOND EDITION, AUGUST 2012

ISBN 978-0-578-11084-4

Edited by Jennifer Thomas

Cover Design by Kate, Ink – www.kateink.com

Author Photo by Alicia E. Barrón – www.aliceinpictureland.com

Acknowledgments

For Mamá, Papá, Chube, Alicia, Ferni, Belli and Sebas – my grounding roots, my inspirational nourishment, my most flavorful and cherished blessings.

❉

My most sincere thanks to Kevin Knox, Julie Sheldon Huffaker and Kenneth Davids for the most entertaining, enjoyable and fascinating introduction into the world of coffee and for helping me appreciate the gift that coffee is, the joy that it brings to people and, in Mr. Davids' words, the encouragement to community that its gentle intoxication generates.

Enjoy.

1

Every social lubricant has its home away from home, its church, as it were, where its effects are celebrated in public ceremonies and ritual conviviality. – Kenneth Davids

Long before the Café Olé there was Doña Pilar's Café. There was no fancy logo, no clever or catchy name for it. Only twelve bright-blue, hand-painted block letters -- CAFÉ CON LECHE -- embellished the exterior walls of the white cement-block building on the northwest corner of Terrace Avenue and Elm Street in Nogales, Arizona. The letters moved in a slight downward slope across the top-left side of the structure and I never stopped to question it. It never occurred to me, despite my constant search for balance and linearity, that they needed fixing. In fact, any attempt to align or straighten them for the simple sake of aesthetics would have been an affront to Doña Pilar and her café.

Over the years, I had learned Doña Pilar's philosophies on life. She always spoke in parables and whether she talked about love, life, beauty, hardship or anything else, coffee was invariably the common factor in all of her stories. "A coffee bean can be gorgeous to look at," she would say whenever some overly primped type would stop by the café, "so shiny and even that it almost looks artificial, but even the most impressive of coffee beans can taste like shit."

She had a deep and raspy voice from years of cigar smoking and her speech carried an exotic blend of Spanish, French and English intonations that she had picked up over the years. Pilar Bontecou had been born in Tapachula, Chiapas, in Mexico. Coffee and its cultivation had percolated into the core of her being long before she was even born. Her father, Renaldo Bontecou, had been a Haitian-born, French-African mulatto. At age fifteen, during the U.S. occupation of Haiti, Renaldo had migrated west following the coffee trade into Santiago de Cuba and then eventually into Tapachula in Chiapas.

In Tapachula he worked in La Moka, a coffee plantation named after the mythical city in Arabia where the commercialization of coffee began back in the ninth century. La Moka was well known for its high-grown (*altura*) coffee, which had a distinctive milk chocolate, nutty flavor to it. In smaller quantities, it also produced the best world-class coffee Mexico had to offer. With great acidity and deep flavor intensity, the *Perla de Xoconostle*, La Moka's trademark crop, yielded a drink experience not easily matched by other coffees.

Like the history of the coffee bean, brimming with intrigue, passion and enchantment as it made its way from Abyssinia (now known as Ethiopia) into India and finally across the Atlantic into the Americas, Doña Pilar's story did not want for drama. She was born in 1935 to her then-twenty-five-year-old agriculturist father and his paramour, the German wife of the owner of La Moka. Although rumors of their love affair had circulated throughout the plantation for years, it was on the night that Pilar was born, with her dark French-roast complexion, that the rumors were confirmed. It was not quite ten full days after she was born that La Moka was sold off to an American agricultor by the name of Robert Mitchell. After that day, neither Renaldo nor Pilar ever saw the woman who gave birth to her again.

Doña Pilar grew up in the coffee plantation with her father. Raised around French, Mestizo and Native Indian workers, she learned to speak French, Spanish and even a bit of the regional Nahuatl dialect. She also learned to smoke cigars and play cards to a fault but, most importantly, she learned the secret to the cultivation and preparation of the finest Mexican coffee. Perfecting the more than seventeen labor-intensive steps required to fill coffee mugs throughout the world became Doña Pilar's craft.

"Coffee beans are like people, *querida*," she would always tell me. "They must be properly cultivated if they are to be any good. And coffee, it's like love. The entire world has learned to drink it, but only a few know how to brew it."

Since the age of twelve, Doña Pilar had been in charge of wet-processing the coffee beans at La Moka. After the farmers carefully hand-plucked the ripe cherry fruits from the fifteen-foot-high evergreen shrubs, wet-processing, which involved large fermentation tanks, was used to free the coffee beans or pits from within. A total of four layers surrounded the coffee bean: a shiny outer skin, a sticky pulp, a stiff parchment casing and a thin silverskin that clung to the bean. During fermentation, the smell of fresh-made wine filled the air and the sticky pulp swelled up and loosened around the coffee bean. If fermentation was not stopped at the exact moment when the enzymatic reaction was complete, the coffee beans began to rot quickly. It was precisely due to the sensitive nature of this task that Robert Mitchell had hand-picked Doña Pilar, the most experienced worker at the coffee plantation apart from her father, for that job.

After fermentation, the beans were freed from the loosened pulp and laid out to dry three feet off the ground on Parijuela beds under the sun. They were raked and turned regularly throughout the day to make sure that they dried evenly. The next step was milling the coffee beans. Using nothing but their bare hands, the plantation workers removed the stiff parchment casing and the thin silverskin from the beans. Lastly, they would filter out any debris or broken beans and sort the remaining ones by size and density to ensure good roasting. The end result was raw coffee, or what people in the coffee trade referred to as green beans.

Doña Pilar knew that under the right storage conditions, raw coffee could produce a flavorful and aromatic cup even one year after being stored. The trouble with green beans, however, was that they required a lot more work when turning them into a cup of coffee. They had to be properly roasted and ground before they could be brewed. Unlike the Café Olé and most other popular coffee houses, Doña Pilar stored only green coffee in her café. She never kept old stock, either. Her coffee was never more than three to six months old. She was also very particular about storing her raw coffee. In order to avoid direct sunlight, mold, bugs and larvae, she had adapted her basement so that the temperature was always between 65 and 70 degrees Fahrenheit and the humidity levels were never higher than fifty percent. While large commercial roasters vacuum-packed their green coffee in airtight plastic bags, Doña Pilar knew that condensation could rot the green coffee over time and, therefore, used only high-quality vegetable-treated burlap sacks to allow the coffee beans to breathe.

Doña Pilar left La Moka in Tapachula and arrived in the American border town of Nogales, Arizona, in 1955. By the time she reached adolescence, her skin had turned a light-mocha color and her eyes, like her father's, were a deep, mesmerizing hazel. She had a strong, robust figure and her arms, like the rest of her body, had a natural contour to them. It was Pilar's foreign beauty and her exotic charm that captivated the hearts of many during her youth. Among those captive was James Mitchell, Robert Mitchell's oldest and married son.

Not unlike the woman who had given birth to her, Doña Pilar, at age twenty, found herself just days past childbirth and on her way out of La Moka. She had been working in the coffee mill close to nightfall when Robert Mitchell approached her. Her father, Renaldo, stood by his side. Her womb was still tender from childbirth and her chafing fingers throbbed as she picked and peeled away the hardened parchment from the coffee beans. Robert Mitchell's face was bleary. Dark circles under his eyes were evidence of the sleepless nights that he had endured over the past weeks. Pilar knew that over the years, Robert had come to see her and her father not only as an asset to the plantation but also as friends. They had been his right hand while his own family had shown no interest in the plantation. Pilar also knew, however, that the economic stability of the plantation depended greatly upon James Mitchell's marriage to Martina Aragón, the daughter of the governor of Chiapas. In exchange for Pilar's disappearance and silence, Robert arranged for her and her baby daughter, Beatriz, to enter the United States. As a means for survival, Pilar negotiated another deal with Robert Mitchell. Every year she was guaranteed 300 pounds of La Moka's seasonal supply of *altura* coffee and 150 pounds of their best crop, the *Perla de Xoconostle*.

I was in seventh grade when I first started visiting Doña Pilar's Café on my own. Beatriz was thirty-two. By six o'clock every morning, she was already carrying tray after tray of steaming terra cotta mugs from one end of the café to the other. While she made her way among the mahogany round-top tables, the conical burr grinder, the stove-top kettle, the milk steamer, the coffee press and a small espresso machine, Doña Pilar roasted fresh coffee beans in the back.

The degree of roast that Doña Pilar applied to her green coffee was always relative to the potential of the particular coffee that she was working with. "Green beans are only seeds of potential flavor," she would say. "Just like people, they cannot be pushed into becoming what's not in their nature. Apply too much heat and they'll char. Apply too little heat and they'll lack body and substance. The trick is finding the level of roast that brings out the best in the coffee bean, the perfect path for the bean to express itself."

A doorway behind the cash register led to the room where Doña Pilar had installed her gas-fired roasting machine. The contraption looked very much like an oversized clothes dryer. Every morning Doña Pilar would pour the green coffee into the barrel-like cylinder that spun and heated the coffee beans. Using time, temperature, sight, smell and sound to gauge the roasting process, Doña Pilar became a true artisan roaster.

During the first few minutes in the process, temperature rose to about 212 degrees Fahrenheit. At that point water began to boil and evaporate. Next, at about 266 degrees, sugars in the coffee began to decompose. After three or four minutes, the beans turned bright yellow and began to give off a grass-like smell. Just past the seven-minute mark, the beans turned a light tan and the first pop took place, leaving the beans puffed up to twice their original size like popcorn. At that point, Doña Pilar would slightly lower the temperature. Sometimes she would stop the process there for those customers who liked a basic light-cinnamon roast.

For the more adventurous customers, she would continue until the beans turned a light brown then a reddish brown as they approached Classic Full City roast. At Full City roast, the coffee beans acquired the highest possible body (the weight and feel of the coffee on the tongue), while still possessing maximum acidity (a vibrant, fruity crispness) and aroma. This was by far the most popular roast at Doña Pilar's Café.

For a few of her more audacious customers, Doña Pilar went even further in the roasting process. Twelve to thirteen minutes into it, she would begin to listen for a hissing sound that denoted the arrival of a second pop. The second pop was basically the shattering of the beans' cell walls. The natural oils inside the beans would begin to move up to the surface and a sweet, caramelized-sugar taste took over. That was Vienna roast.

Finally, for only a handful of her patrons, my mother included, Doña Pilar would go into the last and most extreme realms of the roasting process: Italian and French roasts. At Italian roast, the coffee beans exhibited a deep, dark brown, shiny coat. At French roast, they were pretty much jet black. The smoky taste of the coffee at that extreme state was more an indication of the power of the roast than of the original green bean.

After reaching the desired roast, Doña Pilar would open the door on the front part of the roasting machine and spread the beans evenly onto a ventilated cooling tray. After they cooled off, she would store them in airtight containers that were also kept in the cool, dark and dry basement but never for too long. It was usually only a matter of hours before Beatriz took them back up for grinding.

When Doña Pilar was not roasting, she spent most of her time behind the cash register smoking cigars, playing *naipes* and drinking her own coffee concoctions. School let out at 2:45 in the afternoon and by three o'clock, I would already be at the café. In a dried coconut shell, which Doña Pilar said increased the flavor and aroma of the coffee, she would pour me a mixture of steamed milk, cinnamon-roasted coffee and two heaping teaspoons of sugar.

"Coffee is the only thing that really connects people in this world, *mon amour*," she once told me. She often closed her eyes when she spoke, the smoke from her cigar forming a vaporous white screen before her mulatto complexion. Her rhythm was slow and measured. "From Ethiopia to Egypt, the Arabian Peninsula and Turkey, Java in Indonesia, Italy, Marseille in France, London, Berlin, Madrid, Brazil, Colombia, the Netherlands, El Salvador, Venezuela, Guatemala, Cuba, Mexico, the United States, Canada -- you name it. No matter how foreign people's lives may seem, there's always that point of convergence."

She opened her eyes briefly to look at me. The whole time that she had been speaking I'd had the coconut shell stuck to my face. Feeling a little embarrassed, I set it back down on the counter and gave her my full and undivided attention.

"Nothing brings people together like coffee, Nena." Another veil of smoke made its way between us. Her eyes closed again. "Not even love."

For hours, I sat at Doña Pilar's Café savoring her coffee potions and listening to her low-toned, almost lyrical voice talk about ideas, experiences and feelings that I did not yet fully understand. All the same, I listened.

2

There is a very delicate relationship between farming practices and the final quality of a cup of coffee. Several initial factors influence seedling growth and contribute to the resulting flavor, body and aroma of coffee. From plant pedigree to the conditions of cultivation, including temperature, humidity, wind turbulence, sun exposure, latitude, altitude and the nature of the terrain, there is an inherent truth governing the ability of a region to grow good coffee.

On January 1, 1975, U.S. Attorney General John N. Mitchell and former White House aides H.R. Haldeman and John Ehrlichman were found guilty of the Watergate cover-up. On January 6 of the same year, *Wheel of Fortune* premiered on NBC. January 12, the Pittsburgh Steelers defeated the Minnesota Vikings 16 to 6 in Super Bowl IX. February 22, Drew Blyth Barrymore was born to John and Jaid Barrymore. March 4, Charlie Chaplin was knighted by Elizabeth II in the United Kingdom. March 10, *The Rocky Horror Show* opened on Broadway. March 15, Aristotle Onassis died of bronchial pneumonia in Neuilly-sur-Seine, France. Same day, Stacy Ann Ferguson, a.k.a. Fergie, was born in Hacienda Heights, California. April 4, Bill Gates founded Microsoft in Albuquerque, New Mexico. May 16, Japanese mountain climber Junko Tabei became the first woman to reach the summit of

Mount Everest. June 4, Angelina Jolie Voight was born in Los Angeles. June 20, *Jaws*, the blockbuster thriller directed by Steven Spielberg and based on the best-selling novel by Peter Benchley, was released. June 27, Tobias Vincent Maguire better known simply as Tobey, or even better known as Spiderman, was born in Santa Monica, California. July 31, Jimmy Hoffa was reported missing in Detroit, Michigan. August 25, Bruce Springsteen released his third album, *Born to Run*. September 9, Michael Sebastian Bublé was born in Burnaby, British Columbia, Canada. September 15, Pink Floyd released their ninth studio album, *Wish You Were Here*. September 22, President Gerald Ford survived a second assassination attempt. October 5, Kate Elizabeth Winslett was born in Reading, Berkshire, England. October 11, NBC aired the first episode of *Saturday Night Live*. October 22, the Cincinnati Reds defeated the Boston Red Sox to win the World Series. November 10, the SS Edmund Fitzgerald sank 17 miles from the entrance to Whitefish Bay on Lake Superior. December 30, "Cablinasian" golfer Eldrick "Tiger" Woods was born in Cypress, California. Somewhere in between all of that, inevitably affected to some degree by the social, political and environmental vibes of the time, perhaps also by the changing positions of the stars and the planets, I was born in Nogales, Arizona: Ximena Ferrer, more commonly referred to as Nena; 6 pounds 8 ounces; 9:13 p.m.; Holy Cross Hospital.

I was the second child and the first daughter for my parents. My brother, who is three years older, was born with straight, dark brown hair, a pale-white complexion and lungs that could belt out sound perceptible several doors down. My younger sister, born three years after me, was pretty much a female replica of my brother. I, on the other hand, had light-brown, unruly, curly hair, a caramel complexion marked with a darker café-au-lait birthmark on my neck, and an ability to hold back sound that many, beginning with the attending doctors at Holy Cross, found disquieting. It took at least two good, solid spanks to get my lungs blaring nice and loud.

My mother was Mexican. My father was Puerto Rican and I always longed for a clever catchphrase to identify myself with. Unlike Tiger Woods, who used the portmanteau *Cablinasian* to describe his Caucasian, Black, American-Indian and Asian ethnic background, the best that I could find was Mexirican. Not very original, but it worked.

Portmanteau, by the way, referred to a term that merged two or more words (or word parts) to give a new meaning. A common one was *brunch*, breakfast and lunch squished together. *Camcorder* was the portmanteau for camera-recorder. *Fantabulous* stood for fantastic and fabulous. One of my recent favorites thanks to Napoleon Dynamite, *liger*: lion + tiger. At a very young age, exploring such sequences of informational tidbits became somewhat of a pastime for me. Language itself became a diversion. To understand the logic behind that, other than my innate nerd and genetic makeup, one needed to understand the culture and, more specifically, the role of language in Nogales, Arizona.

Looking at a linear map of North America, it was not hard to pinpoint Nogales. The line depicting the border between Arizona and Mexico formed an angle at exactly one point. That point was Nogales. Brushing up against it from the south or, as some would believe, overlapping into it was Nogales, Sonora, Mexico.

In 1853, the United Sates paid Mexico ten million dollars in exchange for a 29,670-square-mile region south of the Gila River and west of the Rio Grande. The Gadsden Purchase, as it became known, delineated clearly the physical division between the newly acquired American territory and Mexico. A chain-link fence and later a virtual fence with radar and surveillance cameras were used to separate the two countries. What the fences could not put a wedge through, however, was the inevitable cultural and linguistic overlap.

During my childhood years, it became next to impossible to notice where English stopped and Spanish began. McDonald's drive-thrus unfailingly took orders in Spanglish. Neighbors scolded in an adult-rated version of Spanglish. Even in school, Spanglish became more and more common. For that reason, it was not unusual to find me with a beat-up Webster's Dictionary in hand. It was a small attempt at making sense of my world.

At home we spoke only Spanish. Although my parents, my brother, my sister and I all spoke near-perfect English, Spanish was the idiom we all naturally broke into when initiating conversation. It was a spontaneous act, no premeditation.

Our inclination toward Spanish was influenced in a big way by the fact that we still spent a lot of time in Nogales, Sonora. On Sundays, it was tradition to spend the day at my grandparents' home. They lived in the same old stone-brick house on the outskirts of Nogales, Sonora, where my mother and her sister had been born and raised. Starting at around eleven o'clock in the morning all the way through the classic Mexican television show *Siempre en Domingo*, which ended at nine o'clock at night, my parents, aunt, uncle, siblings, cousins and I took up residence at my grandparents' house. Most of the adults spent the time on the front porch by the *carne asada* grill. The kids, depending on their age, gender and personality traits, usually opted either for the living room, which had the television set, the bedroom, which had the telephone, or the wilderness of the Sonoran Desert, which stretched out behind my grandparents' property. Despite the uncharacteristic choice for my gender, I ran with the latter group.

My cousin Daniel, whom we all called *Piru*, was my accomplice in mischief. He was almost four years younger than I, but the most compatible by far in terms of temperament and taste. We were always the first to disappear after lunch and the last ones to materialize at the end of the day. One time when we turned up well past our curfew, we were grounded and restricted to the interior of the house for a whole month. For four Sundays in a row, we hid inside my grandparents' closet and leafed through an old Spanish dictionary that my grandfather kept on the topmost shelf. We spent hours looking up all the dirty words that we could think of inside the yellowed pages. *Nalga* was the very first word that we looked up and it was an impish thrill to find it sandwiched between *naipe* and *nan*a on page 675. *Fondillo* was another one. Then there were *pinche* and *cabrón*, both of which, to our amusement, appeared nice and clear on the crinkled pages.

It was on a Sunday, a day after Piru's mom cooked a bad *cabrilla* that kept everyone in her home running to the bathroom for days, that I sat alone inside my grandparents' closet. A few weeks earlier I'd heard a word from Ramona, my next-door neighbor. Ramona was fourteen at the time, two years older than me, and always talked about boys. She wore cut-off shorts and skimpy tops with spaghetti straps that sometimes fell off her shoulders revealing soft, brown skin all the way from her underarms to the center of her developing breasts. She was regularly suspended from junior high school for kissing and rolling around on the football field with her boyfriends during lunch hour. While most of the neighborhood kids walked home from school, Ramona would sit outside her house flirting with the boys as they passed by and talking smack with her girlfriends, who were always interested in hearing about her embellished sexual adventures. "It was orgasm after orgasm," I'd heard her say. By the expression on her face (eyes shut, lips puckered) and by the circular motion of her hips atop a rusted folding chair, I sensed that *orgasm* was another good dirty word to look up in my grandpa's dictionary.

The smell of grilled *arracheras* filled the air while I sat underneath the cedar-wood closet shelf, thumbing through the loosened pages in the dictionary. I found it on page 703.

ORGASM (ôr'găz'əm) **n.** Maximum point of sexual excitation characterized by strong feelings of pleasure and by a series of involuntary muscle contractions including genital and feet muscle spasms. It is also accompanied by other organic transformations including increase in tension, tachycardia and occasional loss of consciousness which can oftentimes lead to the verbalization of illogical utterances.

For some reason, I did not find that word to be funny. It wasn't like *fondillo* or *pedorro*. No, it was a very different feeling that came over me as I sat cramped inside my grandparents' closet that Sunday. It was like the feeling that I'd had when I saw Ramona thrust her pelvis back and forth on the chair. Or like the feeling that I got every time I sat atop the highest monkey bar on the school playground. It was a feeling of danger and mischief mixed in with a sweet, addictive pleasure. It was a new feeling, a puzzling one. Maybe it was that mishmash of emotions that made people lose touch with reality and speak words of nonsense, I thought. That day I decided that whenever those feelings came upon me, I would speak as little as possible. I had always been one to direct my feelings and thoughts inward (a full-blown introvert according to psychologist Carl Jung's standards) and now there was one more reason to do just that. I would not willingly make a fool of myself.

When my grandma opened the closet door to look for a sweater, I was sitting on the floor, a little short of breath and hugging the bulky dictionary to my chest.

"Good Lord, Nena." She pulled me up and placed the dictionary back on the shelf. "Only you get this excited over an old dictionary. Come on now. Come spend some time with the rest of the girls in the front room." She dragged me outside.

It was at least fifteen minutes before I talked to anyone, just to be on the safe side. While I sat half-mindedly watching Raúl Velasco with a bad comb-over and glasses that were too big for his face on TV, I decided one more thing. I would never believe anyone who talked to me in that strange emotional state either. No, I knew better than that. I would not believe them.

3

Monday, February 24, 2003

The line inside the Café Olé already trailed back toward the restrooms when I walked in that morning. It was a quarter past eight. I had meant to arrive earlier, but my alarm clock had not gone off. Normally, I beat the clock by around a minute or so. It was set at 6:15 a.m. and most mornings I woke up instinctively at 6:14 just before the buzzer went off. Since my twenty-eighth birthday, my internal clock had gotten even better. Sometimes, maybe two or three mornings in a row, I would wake up at exactly the same time, down to the very same second. The previous night, however, I'd had too many things on my mind and setting the alarm clock had not been one of them.

Initially, I had planned a quiet Sunday evening at home with Mimi, my fourteen-year-old Scottish Terrier who was half-blind and could do little more than eat, sleep, bump into walls and poop. The 45th Annual Grammy Awards were on that night so I had prepared a nice assortment of high-calorie snacks and chilled a bottle of red wine. Although John Mayer, Norah Jones and Coldplay were set to headline my evening, twenty minutes into the big show, a big dollop of drama ended up taking center stage. To top it off, my usually fine-tuned internal clock had also gone haywire on me and it was 7:17 a.m. before I first cracked my eyes open in the morning.

I had been living in Tucson for ten years already. Three days after high school graduation, I moved out of my parents' home in Nogales and started a summer course at the University of Arizona. Ironically, I was the first among my classmates to leave for college yet the only one who still had no clue as to what I wanted to study. Truth was that I had applied and gotten into college not necessarily because it was a deep inner calling for me, but because it seemed the right thing to do and, in all honesty, it had not been all that hard. Many things in my early life seemed to happen that way. I was used to accomplishing things without really being aware of the process.

At the end of four years, I had a Bachelor of Science degree in psychology and three years later a Ph.D. in psycholinguistics. Now it wasn't that I did not suffer through endless hours of homework, studying for exams, doing research, writing papers and presenting a dissertation, it was just that I didn't necessarily mind doing the work. The only way I could explain it, contrary to my friend Sasha's theory that I was profoundly disturbed and had a severe masochistic personality, was to say that I experienced exactly the opposite of what people diagnosed with attention deficit disorder experienced. While impulsiveness, hyperactivity and a short attention span were an intricate part of their lives, I very much enjoyed sitting back and analyzing things to a pulp. It was an inherent part of me. I could literally sit for hours and just observe situations and people as they sat on their own or walked by or conversed and interacted with others. Studying the smallest of things in people's behavior, voice intonations and language inflections, of course, but also unrhythmic inhalations or subconscious facial expressions, such as an eye or a lip twitch, became a passionate hobby for me. It was that ability to sit still and take in the world and not some über intellectual aptitude that made it possible for me to focus and finish the things that I started without too much hoopla or ceremony.

For three years, since officially becoming a Doctor of Philosophy, I had been working at the university, investigating how children acquired their first, second and, in some cases, third or fourth languages and what role cultural environment played in all of that. Although my always-too-blunt pal Sasha had always been very vocal about how she would rather shoot both of her big toes off than do what I did for a living, I actually enjoyed my work. Still, I needed a good kick of caffeine to start off my mornings and being seventy miles away from Doña Pilar's Café had left me no choice but to resort to the commercial coffee of the Café Olé. Yes, preparation was mostly relegated to a machine and the "baristas" seemed more invested in looking the part than mastering their coffee-making skills (matching Café Olé baseball cap and apron, perky ponytail, overly animated facial gestures, overly enthusiastic yet completely uninteresting conversation), but there was, after all, a Café Olé (sometimes two or three) on practically every block. It was the ultimate example of convenience over quality that made Doña Pilar break out into hives.

The overpowering smells of vanilla and hazelnut (the two most popular flavors used to disguise bad coffee) filled every corner in the crammed coffee shop on the southwest corner of Speedway Boulevard and Silverbell Road. In the sitting area, all I could see were open newspapers held up by body-less hands. As my eyes swept the shop a bit further, I immediately spotted Lalo standing next to the counter by the espresso machines. He was next in line to order. As if on cue, he turned around and caught me staring at the back of his head. Oftentimes, I really wondered whether it was possible to attract an unsuspecting person's attention simply by staring at them. Unfortunately for me, it always seemed to happen with people that I didn't want it to happen with. I had tried averting my eyes quickly, but it had been too late. He was already waving for me to go to the front of the line with him. Any other day I would have refused. I hated when people cut in front of me. It was one of the few things, along with people slurping or chewing their food noisily, that I just could not tolerate. My ears would burn and my mouth would go dry. Besides, I was never too enthused about socializing with Lalo, especially not that early in the morning. I just didn't have the energy to try and follow along with one of his multifaceted conversations or play the tit-for-tat game that he always seemed to enjoy playing with me. Plus, he always looked at me as if he knew something about me, some big secret that no one, not even I, was aware of. It made me terribly uncomfortable. I liked being the observer, after all, not the observed. But I *was* running more than an hour late and time-wise I could not afford to turn down his offer.

"Almost there?" I walked over casually as if I had been standing there before and had only walked away momentarily. I felt a dozen eyes pierce holes in the back of my head.

"Almost," Lalo replied. His olive-green eyes fixed on me and a sarcastic smile curled the corners of his fleshy lips. "Running late?"

"Yep." I focused on a skinny blonde manipulating the steamer lever on one of the espresso machines. I could never look at Lalo straight in the eye. The worst part was that he knew that.

"Were you up late last night?" he continued.

"Little bit." Skinny Blonde was now sprinkling cinnamon onto a frothy cup of something.

"Did you have company?" A small pause, but not long enough for me to even begin enunciating a response. "I heard Alex is in town."

Lalo's timing and semantics were always impeccable. It was practically impossible to sidestep his insinuations. I turned to face him. I knew he could read me like an open book, but I still made an effort to lie. "Yeah, I heard he's in town, too, but, believe it or not, Alex has nothing to do with the fact that I'm running late. I can manage to make myself late for work without anyone's help." I inhaled at least two unrhythmic breaths.

Lalo's cynical smile widened and I regretted having jumped to the front of the line with him. I should have stayed in the back near the restrooms. There I wouldn't feel as transparent and as vulnerable as he always made me feel.

Skinny Blonde took to the register. Lalo ordered a moyenne, skinny mocha. *Moy*enne, by the way, was pronounced "mwa-yén" and not "moy-yeen" as most people did. It meant medium in French and, in my opinion, was just an attempt by the Café Olé to seem exotic. They perpetuated the custom of using a foreign language to describe serving size although, at the end of the day, whether it was grand or large, petit or small, moyenne or medium, their coffee was simply *moyen* (mwa-yé~/ *Fr.* **adj.** average).

While Lalo paid and flirted with Skinny Blonde, I took a few deep breaths and appreciated being away from his critical eye. The palpitations on my right temple eased up a bit and my shoulders lowered to their normal position. Half-mindedly, I turned to look at the people standing in line behind me. I could have sworn I saw smoke coming out of at least two people's ears. I was turning to face forward again when a short, fat woman in a tight, burgundy twill skirt-suit (which made her look like a smoked sausage) took charge.

"What? You think we di-in't notice?" Her voice had the trademark *pocho* accent (listen to the Latin Kings of Comedy in your mind's ear). As usual, I said nothing. The palpitations quickly started to rev up again. "Just 'cause phlegm-eyes wants to git in your pants..." Smoked Sausage continued. Shoulders were now touching ears. The steamer hissed furiously across the counter and heat started to run up the middle of my back, past my nape and onto my scalp. Before Lalo could turn to continue the torture, I cut out of the line and jetted out of the coffee shop.

The pounding in my ears was deafening as I walked toward the parking lot, shuffling through my purse to find the car keys. I hated confrontation. Besides, Lalo did not want to "git" in my pants. As a matter of fact, he barely liked me. He was always trying to make me feel shallow and uncultured. I wasn't his type, either, not physically nor intellectually. Physically, he leaned more toward the extremes, skinny blondes or voluptuous dark-skins. I was comfortably average. In the coffee world, you could say I was a Full City or a Vienna roast (medium brown, medium body, balanced flavor and aroma). Looking at his relationship history, it was clear that he was more into the Light Cinnamons (light tan, unpleasantly sour, little or no body) or the more audacious French roasts (dark brown, full body, bold flavor).

Intellectually, we were also in two different leagues. Other than language and a few other minor mannerisms, I didn't care to critically analyze every aspect of people's lives: their taste in music, movies and books; their choice in haircuts, fabrics or food; their preference between Safeway, Albertson's or Food City. It made no difference to me. Lalo was always trying to find some deep political or philosophical explanation for everything. If someone farted, he quoted Aristotle and Kant one right after the other. How ridiculous. How draining.

When I arrived at the psychology building at the university, my face was flushed and my armpits soaked. My research assistant was already waiting along with two "subjects"

[*Def.* **n.** any object or phenomenon that is observed for purposes of research, in human subject research often called a respondent or participant. *Pi.* (or *personal interpretation*) a term used to strip away a layer of humanness from people participating in a research study so as to prevent the researcher from relating with them on a human level, which (heaven forbid) can lead to emotionally contaminated data]. I was more than two hours into my workday, had only slept a measly three hours (definitely because of Alex), and had not even had my morning dose of java. It was going to be a long day.

4

Thursday, September 3, 1987

It was my fourth day in junior high school and although school let out at a quarter to three, I didn't get home until close to five in the afternoon. Junior high had turned out to be a bit more stressful than I had anticipated. The logistics, more so than class content, were what I found most unnerving. Running around between classrooms all day, adjusting to a different teacher for each class, interacting with kids I had never before seen in my life really rattled my nerves. Of course, it did not help that only two days prior I had gotten my period for the first time. For two uncanny days, I'd had to wander about a new school with a bloated belly and a bitter taste of metal in my mouth. Not to mention a wad of "high-absorbency" material between my legs that felt completely unnatural. I had always been a sucker for simplicity and stability and so far junior high school had been neither. Doña Pilar's Café had been, by general admission, a saving grace from insanity for many so on my way home that Thursday I decided to stop in for a while.

It was actually the first time that I went to the café on my own. Usually, I went with my mother, Cecilia. She was a translator and language consultant (and, hence, responsible for half of my nerdy gene pool) and whenever she had a big project to work on, which was most of the time, she would resort to the stimulating milieu of the café. Unlike my brother and sister, who always opted to stay behind with Isela (our live-in nanny, whom I actually did not identify as such until many years later when I realized that not everyone had an Isela prototype living with them), I loved to tag along with my mother. As she worked on manuscript-length documents, I sat and surveyed the comings and goings at the café.

At around 3:30 or 4:00 p.m., people would start to trickle in for the afternoon rush. The first of the afternoon regulars were always Frank Felix, a sixty-some-year-old pawnbroker (or loan shark if sugarcoating was not your thing), and George Konstantinou, a petite, seventy-some-year-old Nogales fixture with cotton-ball hair and excessively bushy eyebrows. They always sat at a table on the north side of the café by the big window. Mostly, they sat hunched over their coffee mugs in silence. Occasionally, they would make a comment or two about the terrible insomnia that they both suffered or the large amounts of medication that they were each on. Otherwise, the only sound coming from their end was the persistent and somewhat hypnotic "ta-ling, ta-ling, ta-ling" of their coordinated spoons stirring nearly gone coffee.

Around the same time, a group of quasi-hippy school teachers wearing socks with sandals and limp blond hair under crocheted hats took over a table on the west side of the café, across from the cash register. Piles of paperwork on their table indicated that they were there on business although I don't recall ever seeing them do anything with the papers.

In the center of the café, sitting at three joined tables, a group of around six to eight Mexican women also met regularly. Unlike the hippies, however, they always wore flashy (albeit cheap) jewelry and offensively bright-colored makeup. Their manner was also unnecessarily loud. It seemed like they were constantly trying to drown each other out with their own individual conversations and, if I studied them for too long, I unfailingly ended up with a headache.

At a table close to the unisex restroom, David, our neighbor from across the street, was oftentimes found working on his latest novel. He had a quiet and gentle air to him that frequently clashed not only with the feel inside the café but also with that of the entire city of Nogales. Nogales seemed much too boisterous and disorderly for him. Nevertheless, he had been living there with his family for five years already and apparently had not only adjusted but was immune to the chaos. He had written his two best-sellers while living in Nogales.

I sat with Doña Pilar at the front counter. It had been almost five days since my mother and I had last been there, but given all the circumstances in my life since, menarche included, it seemed like much longer. Javier Solis' falsetto in *Malagueña* filtered through the babble of the center tables. Doña Pilar looked at me attentively.

"You're feeling all right, child?" The lit cigar between her lips did not move one bit as she spoke. I nodded a brief yes. It seemed like too much of an effort to try and explain the absurdities of adolescence in the late '80s.

Beatriz walked past us with a carafe of Classic Full City roast coffee for the hippies. On her way back, Doña Pilar gave her a pregnant look, which I was not immediately able to interpret. The next thing that I knew, however, Beatriz was placing a hot ginger root tea on the counter for me. "No caffeine for you today, Nena," she said. I looked at her a bit perplexed. "It makes your blood vessels constrict," she added while patting her lower abdomen. Without further explanation, Beatriz went back to her chores. By then, of course, I figured that their covert exchanges had something to do with the painful spasms that I had been feeling just below the belly button for the past two days.

I sat sipping my tea with Doña Pilar for about an hour. We played some hands of *dompe* and, although we didn't say much to each other, by the time I went home I was feeling much better.

At home my mother had made pan-seared chicken with roasted red pepper sauce. I could smell the natural sweetness of the red peppers all the way from the driveway. Although we never had formal family meals (one of our many big no-nos according to traditional American culture), my mom always prepared topnotch dishes. She loved to cook and the rest of us were accustomed to making our way into the kitchen at our own pace and helping ourselves to whatever was on the stove.

When I made it in, my mom and Isela were just about to finish eating. I took a plate from the cupboard, scooped up some fusilli pasta onto it and piled a spoonful of chicken on top. While I ate, Isela, who was in her mid-forties and had never married or had children, went on and on about how Rosa had just learned that she was the long-lost daughter of a wealthy woman on *Rosa Salvaje*. Isela became so enthused talking about her favorite Mexican soap operas that oftentimes she would run out of breath and almost hyperventilate. My mom would follow along politely and then turn discreetly to wink at me. No matter how hard we had tried, my mom and I were too darned cynical to be able to submerge ourselves fully into the *telenovela* culture. It was a trait that we both realized made us complete misfits and terribly boring conversational partners, but so it was. We couldn't help asking the obvious. For example, why was a thirty-five-year-old woman frolicking around with a bunch of prepubescent kids, playing with marbles, climbing over mansion walls, and sporting dirt-ridden sweatshirts and baseball caps while wearing buttloads of makeup? Our inability to look past the blatant inconsistencies made it impossible for us to focus on anything else, the plot included. So several years back we had stopped trying.

After eating, I opened the fridge and took a quick swig from a 2-liter bottle of 7UP. Although my mom rolled her eyes in disapproval, it was Isela who actually scolded me. She was good at keeping us in line and she did not hold back, not even when our parents were around. I had to give her props for that. I put the 7UP bottle back in the fridge and then smacked a wet one on Isela's left cheek. She turned to look at me and tried to keep a straight face. It lasted all of two seconds before a tender smile betrayed her. "You know you love me, Chela," I taunted as I turned to walk away. Before I had made it safely into the clear, I let out an obnoxiously loud 7UP-induced burp. I was on my way to make the rounds throughout the rest of the house when I heard Isela call me *"cochina"* one more time.

My father, who was an architect (and, therefore, responsible for the second half of my nerdy-yet-creative gene pool), was not home yet. He usually did not come home until after seven. Fernando, my brother, was in his bedroom with two friends listening to Mötley Crüe's *Girls, Girls, Girls* album. They were all going through the awkward stage of middle adolescence (characterized by uneven physical growth) and, therefore, each manifested a degree of freak: long legs, big hands, small head; or thick neck, square shoulders, high-pitched voice; or flimsy (and hairless) legs and arms, bulging Adam's apple and big nose. Whatever the combination, their appearances made it evident that they were still smack in the middle of the pubertal morphing process. I peeked in briefly and, as usual, Fernando's bedroom smelled intensely of B.O. and enclosed fart. I moved on quickly.

Down the hall in the TV room my sister, Elena, was eating flower seeds and watching *Midnight Madness* for the umpteenth time. Barf, from the blue team, had just unscrambled some letters to spell out the word "Fagabeefe." Elena barely took notice me. She could recite every line from the movie by heart yet she was still mesmerized every time she saw it. I sat with her for a while and then decided to head back out toward the front yard. I was never really much of a homebody.

Outside, the sun was setting and it painted the landscape a bright orange. The heat was still bouncing off of the pavement, creating transparent waves above it. I walked out barefoot, as usual. I despised wearing shoes and they were always the first thing to come off when I got home. Besides, I was proud of my thick-skinned feet. I could walk over rocks, scorching hot asphalt and almost anything else that came across my path without feeling an ounce of pain. No one else I knew could do that. Not even Piru. One time he had tried to outdo me by climbing barefoot down the desert slope behind our house to fetch a kickball. From a distance all I saw were yucca plants, barrel cacti and tumble weeds so I tried to discourage him. Still, he went down. He had not made it halfway to where the red rubber ball was lodged when he turned into a crying mess, the bottom of a broken bottle stuck to the bottom of his right foot. Inevitably, every time Piru tried to match my tomboyish ways, he ended up hurt and I ended up grounded.

Sometimes when my grandmother would stop by to visit, she would pull out a foot file from her large, saggy purse (where she could have easily fit a midget if she would have wanted to) and force me to lie still while she shaved off layer after layer of thick hide from my heels.

"A young lady should have soft and delicate feet, Ximena. This is a sin!" She would saw away so vigorously that I could have sworn that I saw beads of sweat forming on her perfectly powdered forehead. Little did she know that it would take me only a few days to roughen them up again.

In the middle of our front lawn, my father had installed a two-tier pond fountain. The base around the pond was twenty inches in height and had become my designated sitting area. On the topmost tier, there was a ceramic statuette of a boy mounted on some sort of a barrel from which the re-circulated water poured back down toward the pond. The boy's facial expression, distant yet mocking, had always given me the heebie-jeebies. I was contemplating his blank stare and scraping off a piece of hard skin from my left heel when I heard a door shut loudly. Ramona, my neighbor, raced past my house. Behind her, Prudencio, her stepfather, burst out of the house. His massive humanity moved as fast as it could after her, but his protruding stomach, which I always believed would touch the floor if it weren't contained by the tight wife-beaters that he always wore, kept him from going too far. He took only a few steps before he tripped over an unearthed cable and tumbled to the ground with a resounding thump. He rolled around awkwardly trying to lift himself up in vain. I did not offer to help him. In all honesty, I did not like the man and I could not bare the thought of touching his hands. They always looked dirty and clammy.

I had never liked the way Prudencio treated Ramona. He was always touching her the wrong way, either slapping her across the face and head or pinching her butt and privies. I also hated the way he stared at all the other girls in the neighborhood. Every afternoon he would sit on the same rusty folding chair in his front porch and watch the girls play kickball or jump rope on the street. He would hold a bottle of Sauza in one hand and rub his crotch with the other every time one of the girls turned to look at him. Even before I fully understood what "perv" meant, I knew that Prudencio Vargas was the worst kind of perv out there.

I saw him wriggle on the hot ground a while longer before I decided to run inside and ask for help. Although I secretly loved his helplessness, I knew that things could get ugly and I did not want to feel responsible.

"He had it coming, the fat turd," my mom muttered softly as she walked out with me. I grabbed a hold of her hand. Just like everything else about her, my mother's hands were strong yet soft to the touch. They always smelled of jasmine, too. I had always liked the way my mom's hands looked. She never bothered with sculptured nails or French manicures. Her nails were always au naturel, clean and trimmed. Unlike most of the other Mexican mothers I knew, she didn't wear a lot of jewelry. She wore a simple-design eternity band on her right ring finger (a Mother's Day gift from my father), a stainless-steel Fossil watch on her left wrist, and a thin, sterling-silver bracelet set with a garnet, an amethyst and a peridot (her children's birthstones) on her right one. Her style was very down to earth and casual and her presence exuded confidence and control. Holding her hand triggered a sense of safety and reassurance.

A small crowd had already started to form around Prudencio, who was still looking like a beached walrus on the ground. Marcela, David's wife, had seen him wobbling on the ground through her living room window. She and her two sons had tried to hoist him up, but when it became too arduous of a task for her and her adolescent boys, a few other people had joined in the effort. As ridiculous as Prudencio looked with a small army of people hovering above him to lift him up, his depravity was still apparent. From the ground he kept reaching for Marcela's hand and ogling every one of her movements. When they all managed to get him back on his feet, he pretended to stumble once more. He stretched out his arms as if to support himself on Marcela, but my mother pulled her away quickly and Prudencio's filthy hands missed Marcela's breasts by a mere two inches as he went back down. His piehole landed on a whitewashed boulder in his front yard that sent his upper-left central and lateral incisors flying out.

When the paramedics arrived almost an hour later, the sun was already starting to set and most people had lost interest and made their way back home although Prudencio still sat on the ground with a bloody mouth. A few people had tried to lift him up a second time, but since no women had participated in the second endeavor he had put little effort into it. Eventually, everyone grew tired and gave up. Before the paramedics lifted him onto a gurney, he turned one last time to where my mother and Marcela stood chatting. He stared long and hard as if waiting for them to acknowledge him. They never did. Standing just off to the side, I looked at him hoping to catch a glimpse of repentance in his face. That never happened either.

Marcela and David had moved in across the street from us just a few weeks earlier. In a short period of time, my mom and Marcela had become quite good friends. Marcela had been born in Poza Rica, Veracruz, Mexico. Like my mother, she was born in the mid-'40s and, therefore, shared not only a lot of cultural but also generational similarities with her. They both came of age during the thick of the social revolution of the '60s and, therefore, had a sense of individuality that did not always sit well with the more traditional folks in our neighborhood. Prudencio, not surprisingly, was one of them. He did not like the fact that my mother and Marcela had no qualms about putting him in his place whenever he tried to get away with some crude sexual remark or inappropriate gesture. He did not like that they could look him straight in the eye while doing it either. Most of all, though, he hated that they could overlook and ignore him with such ease. There was also Guadalupe Cordero (a.k.a. Doña Lupita), Marcela's next-door neighbor who, under the cloak of religious sainthood, disliked and disapproved of practically everything having to do with Marcela and my mother. Me (a.k.a. devil child) included.

Marcela had dark, wavy hair, which she always kept in a loose bun behind her neck. Her olive-colored eyes, however, were what stood out the most upon seeing her. They had an almond shape to them that was delineated further by her dark lashes. In Mexico, her father had been a top government official during the late 1930s when Lázaro Cárdenas, then president of Mexico, had expropriated the petroleum and oil industry in the country. As a result, the Mexican government was given monopoly in the exploration, production, refining and distribution of oil and natural gas. Marcela's father, in turn, was given charge of the Poza Rica oil field in Veracruz, the main source of petroleum in Mexico for decades. Marcela was born the fourth of five daughters and was the only one who married a man who was neither a Mexican nor a hireling of her father's. Her decision to marry David Piercy, an American journalist who did not share her family's love for power and money, brought about a bitter fallout between Marcela and her father. At age twenty-two she moved to the United States with David. For a few years, they lived in El Paso where David's journalistic career as a news broadcaster took off. They later lived in San Diego where his career continued to prosper. Then David left news broadcasting altogether and decided he wanted to write. He had always liked the feel of the border cities so during one of his trips to Arizona, he decided Nogales was where he wanted to write his first novel. Five years, two homes and two best-sellers later, they were still living in Nogales with their fifteen-year-old son, Alejandro, or Alex, and their thirteen-year-old son, Eduardo, or Lalo as everyone called him.

5

*An artfully crafted coffee blend is like a good friendship.
It combines different-origin coffees, each with its own
complementary or contrasting characteristics, and brings forth a
complexity and consistency of flavor that few single-origin
coffees can produce on their own.*

Friday, February 28, 2003

I saw a total of forty subjects that week: sixteen adults
and twenty-four children. Of course, energy-wise, twenty-four
children were equivalent to forty-eight regular-sized people so it
was as if I had really seen a total of sixty-four subjects, more than
three times what was considered reasonable by any researcher's
standards.

If movies were to be believed, my work as a researcher
should have been full of glamour and thrilling, world-changing
discoveries. Perhaps due to the likes of Greer Garson in *Madam
Curie* and other such good-looking and charismatic protagonists
who loomed in Hollywood science flicks, I had always
envisioned myself in a white, pressed lab coat wearing
sophisticated, black-rimmed glasses and jotting down crucial
notes as I observed people through a mirror window from a big
executive office. Instead, the reality of my primarily government-
funded projects were studies done inside my five-by-eight office,
which was crammed with old computers and audio/video

recording equipment that oftentimes broke down halfway through the course of an experiment. Once or twice a month I had access to a functional MRI machine in the Neuroscience Department. Apart from that, however, there was no white coat or fancy glasses or a mirror window or an executive office. In fact, there was practically no money. It was void of any Hollywoodesque glam and excitement yet I still loved doing it.

I loved working with the diverse group of people that came through the university: Jamaican, Puerto Rican, Chinese, Native American, Irish, Greek, Italian, German, Iranian, the whole gamut. One of the downfalls of growing up in Nogales, despite it being an international port of entry, was that you rarely saw anyone who was not Mexican or American or some blend of the two. When you did, they were typically third or fourth generation so their behavior and language were so far acculturated that you could hardly tell them apart from the Mexican and American blends. As Doña Pilar would put it, there was so much variety in their mix that the flavors characteristic of their origin were oftentimes muted. I, for example, had stopped calling buses "*guaguas*" long before I even finished elementary school. In my new Mexican vocabulary they were called "p*eseros*" instead. "*Bizcocho*" was another Puerto Rican term I dropped quickly. I had been at a birthday party at Doña Lupita's house (of all places) when I used the word to describe the birthday cake. "My dad loves to eat *bizcocho*!" had been my exact words. From the ghostly expression on Doña Lupita's face as she covered her daughter's ears, I figured I had somehow managed to push myself a bit further into the realms of hell. When I looked up the word in the dictionary at home, I was mischievously amused to find that in Mexico "*bizcocho*" was a slur word for a woman's genitals. Inadvertently, I had climbed one more notch on Doña Lupita's diabolical list. In the process, I had turned my father into a sexual deviant or a sexual god, depending on which side of the fence you stood.

It was that sort of childlike innocence and that yet uncorrupted use of language that made working with young children especially interesting for me. Their data was not only the most informative in terms of dual language acquisition and processing it was also the most entertaining.

"I'm gonna show you some cards with some pictures on them, okay?" I once asked a pudgy, four-year-old boy who sat across the table from me. He nodded excitedly as he looked back and forth between his mother, who sat next to him, and me. "You're gonna tell me what you see, all right?" More enthusiastic nodding.

The first card showed a cartoon image of a glass with a blue liquid splashing out of it. "*Agua!*" Pudgy responded.

"Good. What do you do with it?" I questioned.

"You drink it… like when you're thirsty."

The next card showed three books stacked one on top of the other. The topmost book lay open. "A book!" Pudgy's reaction time was under the second mark.

"Okay. What do you do with it?"

"You use it to read stories!" His excitement escalated with each response.

The next card showed a red apple. Without hesitation, Pudgy called it out, "It's an apple!"

"And what do you do with it?"

"You eat it!"

The fourth card was an image of a peach. As expected, Pudgy stared at that card a bit longer than the first three. A few milliseconds passed. Then a few full seconds. Finally, Pudgy responded, his enthusiasm receding slightly to give way to a bit of uncertainty, "It's a... it's a food."

"What do you do with it?"

"Well..." full-blown confusion took over Pudgy's face as he pondered over the image a while longer. "I think you're also supposed to... um... maybe it's a butt-crack." His mother almost cracked her neck as she turned to look at him. Blood rushed to her face but before she could say anything, Pudgy finished his task. "You use it to poop!"

I turned the card toward me and sure enough a rosy, ass-like peach (no stem or leaf to help illustrate it) stared back at me. So it went for another twenty-six flash cards. Even though they drained every last drop of energy in me, the kids were by far the best part of my job.

I left the office at around a quarter past six that Friday. Everyone else had left at least two hours earlier so I was the one to shut down all computers and equipment and wash the coffee percolator in the waiting hall. Normally, I would not have minded doing it. Unlike other professors and project directors in the department, I didn't find the chore demeaning or below my level and status. Besides, I did it at home all the time along with cleaning the toilet and Mimi's poop. That particular day, however, I had to be at the airport by 6:30 so as I scrubbed the oily residue from the bottom of the stainless-steel percolator case, I couldn't help but cuss out the lazy, common sense-deficient, NPR-listening wannabe scholars in the department.

Typically, I was not one to curse much. Discipline and self-restraint were two things that I practiced every minute of the day. I didn't like to wear my emotions on the surface, not when I was happy, not when I was angry or sad. Defense mechanism? Maybe. But I was good at it. Most people couldn't figure me out. Except for Lalo, of course. And Sasha. Sasha was the only person who truly knew me inside and out. She could tell what I was thinking simply by looking at me, not a single word needed to be uttered between us. Who would have thought that that girl was so darned smart?

I hadn't seen Sasha in nearly four months. She had been living in Las Vegas for almost five years already. Since she had made it onto Donn Arden's *Jubilee!* at Bally's, she only made it back to Tucson maybe two or three times a year. When she did, she never stayed long. This time she was visiting through the weekend only. I needed to see her.

I arrived at the airport at 6:35 p.m. She flew America West first class and was one of the first to come through the arrivals tunnel. Ever since she had secured her willing-to-go-topless showgirl salary, she had stopped flying coach. In fact, her previous two trips had been on a private jet belonging to Lorenzo Saracini, a forty-seven-year-old fat Italian entrepreneur with lots of money and just as many addictions. His most recent addiction was Sasha.

He had first met her at one of the post-show bashes he threw for new *Jubilee!* cast members at his Spanish Hills Estates mansion. Although during the show Sasha looked just like the other one hundred or so girls who masterfully flashed never-ending faux smiles, lots of Big Bird yellow feathers, bulky, peacock-looking hats, rhinestone-decked g-strings and lots and lots of skin, off stage she undeniably stood apart. She was 5'9" tall, had legs that just wouldn't end and possessed the perfect amount of curvature (for a Latina body, anyway) in all the places where curves were meant to exist on the female form. Her irises were a deep, dark-chocolate color so at a glance her eyes oftentimes appeared to be black. She always kept her straight, black hair at least shoulder-blade length so that she could easily slick and pin it back for the shows. Unlike most of the other Latino dancers, Sasha did not try to conceal or camouflage her dark caramel skin. Sennine skin-bleaching products and Isa Knox lightening foundation were two things never to be found in Sasha's dressing room station. It was for that reason – her unwavering ability to feel comfortable in her skin and, more importantly, her enviable ability to piss on anyone who tried to make her feel inferior – that she stood out the most before Lorenzo Saranici's eyes.

She walked off the plane wearing dark Chanel sunglasses and a stylish gray knit beanie that offset her thick black mane. Her vintage-wash Versace blue jeans paired with a white peasant tank top and a multi-color floral scarf simultaneously accentuated her impeccable round curves and her smooth, dark brown skin. Upon seeing her you couldn't help but feel like you were looking at the "Just Like Us!" feature of Us Magazine. Even though her disguise gear seemed hardly necessary (after all, she was not at all well known outside of her Las Vegas social circle except, of course, for a few drunks who still remembered her from the Tecolote Bar in Nogales), with Sasha the toned-down celebrity style seemed appropriate. It went with her personality, that so-close-yet-unreachable trait that had always been part of her makeup. Besides, her presence definitely gave the ever-so-boring Tucson International Airport a much-needed oomph. In the time that it took for her to get from the secured-off section of the arrivals gate to where I stood, I saw at least four different people do a double take. One person (not surprisingly a male) even went so far as to approach her. Once he was standing directly in front of her, though, he couldn't figure out what to say and ended up turning around and walking away awkwardly.

That was one of the reasons why Sasha and I had always clicked so well. While I despised being noticed (an indication of my "commitment phobia," according to my social psychology class-assigned readings), Sasha thrived under the spotlight. Whenever we went anywhere together, she knew how to draw all the attention toward her. Whether it was her walk, a subtle laugh or a perfectly coordinated glance, she knew how to make everyone around blend into her background, me included. Even if it was, in fact, due to my fear of loss or rejection by others, I reveled in my anonymity next to Sasha.

As she came closer to me, I could see the outline of her mouth widen into a warm smile. She had the most genuine smile of anyone that I knew. It really wasn't difficult to see why she had such a dizzying effect on people, men and women alike. Even old hags like Doña Lupita, who had always used Sasha as her token scapegoat for all of her own daughters' naughty misdoings, had a serious obsession with Sasha. Sometimes I even contemplated the idea that deep down Guadalupe Cordero may have seriously had a crush on Sasha. Hidden behind her religious front, behind her constant and oftentimes illogical biblical recitations, I truly suspected that the woman lusted after Sasha. If not sexually, at the very least she lusted after her natural verve and carefree spirit.

Sasha stretched out her arms and kissed me once on each cheek, a habit she had picked up from Manolo, the Spanish man whom she had lived with before getting her own place in Las Vegas. It felt good to hug her. She smelled of Lolita Lempicka and her skin was warm.

"I've missed you," she said.

"Me too." I continued to hug her. I knew my neediness was glaring, but with Sasha it didn't matter. "How was your flight?"

"Good," she said as she hooked her left arm onto my right one and prepared to walk toward baggage claim. "It was not as good as flying on a private jet, of course, but it was definitely better than coach."

I smiled knowingly. "Yeah, I was gonna ask. The Italian buddha didn't come through this time?"

Her smile slowly melted off of her face. "He offered," she said. "I just didn't accept this time."

We took the escalator down. I stood one step behind her as we effortlessly descended toward ground level. Although she was facing forward, from my angle to her left I could see her lower jaw tense up. A few short seconds later, her throat started to jerk up and down and out of nowhere a fat tear rolled down her left cheek.

"I want to see him, Nena." Her voice was so choked that I could barely make out what she had said. I stared at her with what must have been the face of an imbecile because when she turned to look at me, frustration swept across her suddenly tear-drenched face. "Nico!" she bawled, "I have to see him!"

My apparent stupidity had come about not because I had not known whom she was talking about. I knew exactly whom she had meant. Instead, my confusion had arisen out of sheer shock. After so many years, I had not been expecting Sasha to bring up the subject of Nicolas.

Nico was thirteen years old and had not seen Sasha since he was four. Inez had always made sure that neither Sasha nor anything having to do with her was ever brought up around her grandson. I was the closest link that Inez allowed and it was probably because of that that Nico was so attached to me. Out of respect for Inez's wishes, I never talked about Sasha with Nico either. In a way, it really wasn't necessary. Her presence was implied regardless of whether or not her name was mentioned. The way Nico wrinkled his eyebrows whenever he was confused about something, the way he chortled at a stupid joke, the way he stared into infinity while lost in thought, it was almost as if looking at Sasha herself. Nico must have also sensed some degree of Sasha in me because ever since he had been a little boy, he had always shown a great deal of closeness and familiarity with me. While watching TV or eating or doing any other kind of sedentary activity, he had always liked to sit on top of me and intermittently reach back his chubby arms and interlock his fingers around my neck. He did it with a spontaneity and a sense of safety that he never showed around anyone else, not even Inez.

At thirteen he was still as close to me as when he was a little child. The baby fat was gone, his voice had deepened (except for a few runaway squeaks) and his forehead and chin had started to break out, yet he would still curl up next to me like a kitten in need of attention every time that I saw him. Sometimes as I watched him from a distance, sitting across the room or staring absentmindedly into the television set, it blew my mind to realize just how big he had gotten and how quickly time had passed (a feeling that seemed evermore present since I had hit the latter half of my twenties). It seemed as if it had only been yesterday that Inez and I had chased him around her house and conned him into the shower. As we both struggled to hold him down, he would squirm his naked little body out of our grasp and run away again, leaving behind only the view of a chocolate-chip-like mole on his jiggly butt and the unmistakable smell of six-year-old ass.

In many ways it really had been as if Nico was my own son. I was there the day that he was born. I was there the day that he first went to school and the day that he first punched a kid's tooth out on the playground. I was there the day he successfully spelled the word "geusioleptic" to win the school district spelling bee. I knew almost everything there was to know about him (how he loved ranch dressing, how he had a huge crush on Kirsten Dunst and loved Linkin Park, how he could watch *Overboard* and *About A Boy* over and over again without growing tired of them, how he liked to leave the door open when he went to the bathroom and how he had to sleep with the television on), yet I had no clue as to how he would react to the news that his real mother wanted to see him. After ten years, Sasha wanted to see him.

Sasha had been just shy of sixteen when she found out that she was pregnant. Just over a year and a half before that, she had run away from home. Thanks to her towering height (especially in comparison to the 5'2" average Mexican female), her artistic use of makeup and the availability of authentic-looking fake ID cards just a short walking distance from the border, she had had no trouble landing a job as a bartender at the Tecolote Bar at just fourteen and a half.

Thanks to her alcoholic stepfather, Sasha had mastered many of her cocktail-mixing skills by the tender age of eleven. Hanging out at Doña Pilar's Café (another habit we both shared) had also given her a great deal of insight into the art of combining different ingredients to create one superb drink. Her specialty had always been the *Morena de Fuego*: a quarter ounce of Kahlúa, a quarter ounce of Frangelico, a quarter ounce of Baileys and a quarter ounce of Grand Marnier all combined in a mug with one hot cup of *altura* coffee. Despite the owner's best efforts to make the entertainment portion at the Tecolote Bar the main attraction (namely, a handful of out-of-shape and life-worn women with exotic names waddling about), it was Sasha's charisma behind the bar and her enticing *Morena de Fuego* that kept the ever-growing number of patrons coming back.

Two weeks after she had started working at the Tecolote Bar, Sasha rented a small apartment behind Doña Pilar's Café. It was during that time that I got to know Sasha. She was usually at the café when I stopped by after school. Like me, she always sat at the counter by the cash register with Doña Pilar. Although at first she seemed to make great efforts to ignore me (avoiding eye contact and refusing to engage in any conversations that I initiated), after a week or two she finally gave in. I had been talking to Doña Pilar about rum, the official drink in Puerto Rico, when she joined in out of nowhere.

"There are three shades of rum produced in Puerto Rico -- gold, amber and white." She looked from Doña Pilar over to me. Her gaze was surprisingly soft and gentle. For some reason I had been expecting it to be rather hard and penetrating. "White is the lightest and driest. It can easily take the place of vodka or gin in many drinks." She took only a small breath before continuing. "Amber and gold have a more robust flavor so they're sometimes used to substitute for whiskey. You can serve them straight or on the rocks."

There was a small moment just as she finished speaking when an awkward silence threatened to creep its way in. Fortunately, another one of Doña Pilar's resourceful skills was her ability to weave into any given conversation with effortless grace. A discussion about *Tia Maria*, a Jamaican rum-based coffee liqueur that she had used back in the plantation to prepare a special drink for her father, was the lifeline. After that day, our mid-afternoon get-togethers became somewhat of a ritual. The subjects of our talks became more wide and varied as the days progressed, but from the moment I got to the café after school until it was time for Sasha to start her evening shift at the Tecolote Bar, you could count on the three of us sitting at the counter lost in conversation and coffee.

6

Coffee picking is a crucial step in coffee production and can be a chief determinant for the quality of the end product. Fine coffees, in particular, require utmost care during their harvest. The cherries must be carefully handpicked individually at their respective peaks of ripeness to ensure their optimal flavor.

Friday, September 18, 1987

It was past eight o'clock at night when I saw Inez step out of her house to pick up her mail. It was the first time that I had seen her in over two weeks. Although it was dark out, the dim light from the lamppost across the street was enough to reveal that she still looked a mess. The left side of her face was so swollen that it looked like an overfilled water balloon about to explode. Her left eye was just a long wrinkle lost underneath multiple shades of purple, blue and yellow. Yellow marked the parts of her face where Prudencio's right hook had landed first. Red was typically visible only immediately after Prudencio's fists made contact with her skin. She was usually too dazed and shaky to notice it. A light blue would kick in the following day. Then it was a dark, painful purple that lasted for days, sometimes even weeks. Finally, a greenish tone would take over, then a yellow and then her natural brown tone would slowly begin to reappear. Since Sasha (or Ramona, as Inez still called her) had left, Inez had seen less and less of her brown skin. Prudencio was on a rampage.

Inez had not been the friendliest of people when I first met her. She had been married to Prudencio only a short period of time and was still in the middle of processing her immigration paperwork when we moved in next door to her. Although she was an attractive woman, a toxic combination of low self-esteem, fear of deportation and Doña Lupita's warped propaganda had predisposed her to dislike us, and especially my mother, long before she even met us.

The first time that we saw her it was only from a distance. My mother and I had been unloading boxes from one of the moving trucks when she and Prudencio arrived home after attending 10 o'clock mass. Prudencio's hair was slicked back with so much grease that it oozed down onto his forehead. He wore black polyester slacks, suspenders and a button-down shirt that must have been white at some point but looked a pale yellow. The shirt collar was a darker shade of yellow, almost a brown, and was soaked with sweat and grease. Inez wore a rayon flower-print dress and lilac pumps. While she waited by her front porch, Prudencio walked over to where my mom and I lifted and lowered boxes. Without saying a word, he leaned against the truck bed to watch us work. It wasn't quite five full seconds before he got the first taste of my mother's polite yet unerring bluntness. She set down the box marked "*COCINA,*" placed her hands strategically on either side of her waist, took a full step forward and looked at him casually. "Unless you're here to help carry boxes, you're in the way."

Unaccustomed to overt confrontations by women, it took a while for Prudencio to register my mom's seriousness and for his facial expression to go from morbid perversion to slight confusion to utter stupefaction. Sure of the fact that he was in no way willing or even able to help, he turned around and made his way back to where Inez still stood. As he approached her, he turned once more to find my mother back at work. Unaware that I was still watching, he brought down his right hand across Inez's face. He shoved her into the house, slammed the door behind them and that was the last that we saw of Inez for at least a month.

Even though I told my mother what had happened straightaway, it wasn't until some time later that she approached Inez for the first time. Inez was hostile and defensive like a cornered cat.

"Doña Lupita already told me all about you. You're just looking to make trouble." She intermittently looked up at my mother as she spoke but was never able to hold eye contact longer than a few seconds. "She's told me that you think you're better than us just because you have an education and a fancy job. And with your husband out all the time, you think you can parade around for all the men around here to notice you." Her eyes were back on the ground. "I don't need friends like you."

My mother never took offense to her accusations. Nor did she feel the need to respond or take issue with Doña Lupita.

Instead, she made it clear to Inez that we were available if she ever needed anything.

For well over a year, Inez kept her distance. We saw her only during short spurts of time. Usually it was Ramona or Prudencio that we saw around her house. After Ramona ran away, we didn't see much of Prudencio either. After the day that he landed himself in the hospital with a bloody mouth, the most action that we saw around the neighborhood was Doña Lupita walking from Marcela's house to our house to our other neighbors' houses asking questions about Inez and then filling the void with fictitious stories of her own creation.

"A rotten tree can only produce rotten fruit," Guadalupe Cordero's voice would go down a few octaves every time she recited a holy scripture. "Grapes are not gathered from thorn bushes nor figs from thistles. What else could you expect from that Ramona girl? Just look at her mother."

When I saw Inez by her mailbox that night, I could not care less if she was a thorn bush or a thistle. It hurt just to look at her.

"How are you?" I asked half expecting her to scurry off as usual. She didn't.

"So-so." Her voice was groggy. "How are you?"

"Fine, thank you."

"How's your mother?" Her tone went up a notch toward the end as though she was making a conscious effort to sound friendlier.

"She's doing well, thank you."

"Is she at home?"

"Yes. Would you like to talk to her?"

"No, no. I was just asking." She took quick steps back to her front door. Before she closed the door behind her, she turned once more. Her face looked like a worn-out baseball glove under the porch light. "Good night," she mouthed before disappearing into the darkness inside her house.

After that night, I saw Inez much more often, sometimes up to three or four times a week. It was always after dark. While Laura León (the epitome of the female sex symbol for the not-so-classy, middle-aged Hispanic man) baaed full blast on the stereo speakers, Prudencio spilled out of a brown corduroy reclining chair in the family room. He held a pool stick in one hand (his version of a remote control) and a bottle of Sauza in the other.

"*Yo no soy abusadora, yo no soy...*" Laura Leon's voice gushed painfully out of the house. "*¿Quien será el abusador? ¿Tu o yo? ¿Quien será?*" Exactly two minutes after the agonizing bleating stopped, Prudencio's pool stick would hit the floor and a loud snore filled the air. Ironically, the tequila bottle never fell from his grip. Less than a minute after the deafening snore began, like clockwork, Inez would step out of her house.

At first her conversation was rather generic. A lot of small talk of the how've-you-been, how's-your-mother, how-do-you-like-this-humidity, how-do-you-like-this-heat variety. Every now and then she would slip back into old patterns and allow the subliminal teachings of Doña Lupita to resurge. "It's not natural for women to want to work outside of the home." She would look away whenever she recited any of Doña Lupita's verbiage. "Their only true, God-given responsibility is to tend to their husbands and children. Unless, of course, they're a, you know, D-E-S-B-I-A-N." She always lowered her voice and made exaggerated gesticulations whenever she would spell out a word (albeit incorrectly) for me. Old habits, I guess, were hard to break and, in all honesty, I found it much too amusing to try and correct or alter either her spelling or her cognitive interpretation of things.

Over time, Inez slowly shifted away from her old ways on her own accord. The criticism that she had used to preemptively curb insults that never came from my end was less each time until one day it just stopped altogether. There were also physical changes in her. No more black eyes or busted lips to begin with, at least not for months at a time. Instead there was a glow evident in her dark brown eyes that I had never noticed before. In the safety of our late-night rendezvous, influenced to some extent by the mystical powers of the desert moon, Inez went through a cathartic transformation.

Like my mother, Inez was born in Nogales, Sonora. Unlike my mother, however, Inez was only thirteen years old when she married for the first time. Just seven months later, a few months short of her fourteenth birthday, she gave birth to her first child. When she first told me the story, she made it a point to tell me, more than once, that her baby had been born prematurely. Ironically, until she brought up the subject, I hadn't bothered to do the math. As time passed and as conversations took on a more candid tone, it became clear that she had actually carried her first child full term. Instead, the mismatch in numbers was due to the fact that she had been two months pregnant when she was forced to marry a man thirty years her senior. Whether or not that man was the father of her unborn child I never knew, but by the time Inez turned twenty-five, she was already a widow with five living children and a long history of trauma and abuse in her trodden path.

When we became neighbors, Ramona, the youngest of Inez's five children, was the only one still living with her. Her other four children had left home and, like their mother, had started having babies of their own long before they even made it out of their teens. By the time Inez remarried and moved to the United States with Prudencio, she was a thirty-six-year-old grandmother of eight. A few years later, Ramona would add the ninth.

Despite the many dark episodes in her life, Inez reminisced and focused mostly on the few good ones. She talked a lot about her life as a child, before she turned thirteen. She talked about the quince that grew in her grandmother's backyard, about the smell of fresh-cut pine that filtered out of her grandfather's workshop. Sometimes I thought I saw her eyes water up with emotion as she spoke, but it never lasted more than a split second. Before I could make anything of it, she was already onto something else.

Months passed and although Inez shared more and more about her life each time, she never talked about the physical abuse. The beatings, bruises, open cuts and swollen eyes that

Prudencio had given her over the years never found their way into our conversation. Once, on a warmer than usual early summer night, she made a slight reference to it by comparing herself to Farrah Fawcett in the Spanish-dubbed version of *The Burning Bed*. Before she could say much, though, a loud thump behind us diverted all the attention. In the darkness, a small cloud of dust settled to reveal a frantic Guadalupe Cordero patting the ground on all fours. While eavesdropping from behind a dense row of shrubs that separated our house from Inez's, Doña Lupita had lost her balance and fallen. Her dentures had popped out of her mouth on her way down and lay lost somewhere in the darkness around her. More troublesome than the disappearance of Doña Lupita's poisonous fangs, however, was the fact that the conversation that Inez had initiated for the first time in nine months also went missing that night. Unbeknownst to any of us, it would be a whole year before it would find its way back.

7

Monday, March 3, 2003

I dropped off Sasha at the airport at 5:45 a.m. The temperature had hit 34 degrees Fahrenheit earlier that morning (the lowest temperature to register in Tucson that month) so the atmosphere felt leaden and frigid. Before pulling out of the driveway at home, I had turned on the windshield wipers to try and scrape off or at least thin out the layer of ice that had formed on the glass overnight. The rubber blades, however, didn't seem to do much and, combined with the fact that Sasha had not spoken more than a few words since our drive back from Nogales the night before, the intermittent screeching of the wiper blades on the frozen glass only added to the irritation and heaviness that hung in the air.

On Sunday, I had managed to schedule a quick face-to-face meeting between Sasha and Nico. I didn't tell Inez and, in all honestly, I hated to think of what her reaction might have been if she would have found out that I had been the catalyst for the meeting between her grandson and her estranged daughter after so many years. In a way, I had always believed that deep down Inez wanted them to be reunited. Despite all the ugly words hurled and all the hurt feelings between Inez and Sasha, I truly believed that Inez was longing for an opportunity to mend her family. That argument had been my main mantra as I drove down to Nogales with Sasha in the passenger seat next to me on Sunday. Somehow I managed to compartmentalize the situation in my head in such a way that I felt almost entirely convinced that I was only helping Inez. Without her knowledge or direct participation nonetheless, but I was providing her with that longed-for opportunity to patch things up within her family.

When I first mentioned the possibility of a meeting with Sasha to Nico, he refused. Instinctively, like an unspoken verse he had been practicing and preparing for years, he told me he had no mother other than Inez. His face, however, painted a different picture. His eyes were big with anticipation. His breath escaped hastily up his chest, through his tightened throat and out his open mouth. It was clear to me that he also yearned to see Sasha, but I didn't insist any further. Nico was off limits. I could resort to all kinds of psychological manipulations and ulterior motives to persuade myself into action, but Nico was a different story.

Since he had been a baby, I had taken it upon myself to protect him from the pressures of the rumors and rumblings which inevitably arose after his birth. The first few years, especially, the stories that surfaced were countless and, unfailingly, they were also inaccurate. Fortunately, as time passed and as he grew older, people lost interest until eventually they moved on to more current gossip and left him alone. Now, in his teenage years, I did not want to be the one to influence or pressure him into anything. I was backing out of Inez's house prepared to tell Sasha that the encounter would not be taking place when Nico ran up to tell me that he had changed his mind.

Inez was at mass when I arrived with Nico at Doña Pilar's Café where Sasha had been waiting. I had timed everything so that I didn't have to come across Inez. Honestly, I don't know that I could have kept it from her had I seen her face to face. Even if I didn't fall apart and tell her straightaway, she would have seen it on my face. Over the years she had gotten almost as good as her daughter at seeing right through me.

Sasha sat at a table at the far end of the café, the same table where David had always sat to do his writing. She sat up straight, her hands clasped together on her thighs. The color in her face was gone and her eyes, like Nico's, were filled with a mix of eagerness and dread. She looked completely defenseless. Nico walked in next to me. As we came closer to the table where Sasha waited, I could feel the distance between him and I dwindle until he was pressed tightly against my right side. At one point his moist hand clutched on to mine. When we finally made it all the way toward the back of the café, before anyone had an opportunity to say anything, Nico let go of my hand, turned around and walked out. Sasha and Nico did not exchange a single word.

Throughout the entire drive back to Tucson and the fifteen hours that followed until I dropped off Sasha at the airport, that same thick silence filled the air. As usual, there had been no time for my problems, no opportune moment to bring up that Alex had suddenly come barging into my life again. There had been other things, more important ones that needed my full attention. There was Nico's tender soul in need of protection,

Sasha's guilt-plagued one in need of soothing. There had been no time for my problems. No time at all.

From the airport I went straight to the Café Olé. I arrived just as the doors were opening. Three other people were already waiting outside. One was a skinny, older man in a dark three-piece suit and hat. The other was a woman in her forties with fluffy, long, wheat-colored hair and an indigenous-looking dress with colorful embroidery all along the hem. The third person was Lalo. He was wearing the same khaki pants and pale orange sweater that he had been wearing a week earlier. His pants were so stretched out and saggy at the butt that it was not hard to conclude that they hadn't seen water in weeks. His mane was just a dark mop over his head.

"Morning," he said as he propped open the door with a worn-out brown shoe.

"Hi." I avoided his eyes as usual.

"Making up for last week's tardiness?"

"No. I just dropped off Sasha at the airport. She has a six-thirty flight."

"Ramona?" There was a noticeable change in his tone of voice.

"Yep."

"Is she still living in Las Vegas?"

"Yep." I looked at Lalo for the first time in a long time. A strange vulnerability was perceptible in his face. One I hadn't seen since we were kids in Nogales.

"How's she doing?"

"All right, I guess." I stood behind the woman in the embroidered dress. She ordered a hot chai. Lalo stood in line behind me. Normally I would have found that nerve-racking, but his attention was clearly someplace else. I ordered a large (or *grand*) latté and sat at one of the corner tables. A few minutes later Lalo joined me with a huge (*géant?*) cup of coffee.

"That'll keep you up a good two days," I felt unusually comfortable around him.

"What's she doing in Las Vegas these days?" He ignored my slight attempt at humor entirely.

"Jubilee."

"She's still dancing?"

"Yep."

Lalo looked out the window. The sun came in from the east and brought out the yellow hue in his eyes. That was one thing I always thought Lalo had over Alex. He had the most beautiful eyes. While Alex took after David (his grayish-blue eyes and blond lashes), Lalo was the spitting image of Marcela. He had the same olive-green eyes and the same thick, dark lashes. There was also a penetrating intensity in them that was responsible for my inability to look at him often. It was almost as if he could reach into all the hidden corners inside me that I wasn't quite ready to go exploring yet. On that particular day, though, he was different. Something had thrown him off and he was almost unrecognizable.

Lalo had always been a confusing character to me. Even as a kid in Nogales, he had always embodied a series of contradictions that made it hard for me to dissect and pigeonhole him like I could most other people. For example, he had always been very athletic. He was good at basketball, baseball, soccer and pretty much any other sport in which he partook. At the same time, though, no matter how much I hated to admit it, he was much too bright and articulate to be clumped with the jocks. Another case in point, one that rang true even that very morning at the café, Lalo came from a family that, although not necessarily rich, could easily afford the nicer things in life and certainly the basic necessities. He, however, insisted on wearing the same shabby clothes all the time and rarely invested any money or time on the simplest of grooming practices, a decent haircut for example.

Exhibit number three, Lalo was two years younger than Alex, close to Sasha's age, yet he had always come off as being older. Not physically. As a matter of fact, his smooth, light-caramel skin and soft facial contours had always given him a rather boyish look. Even at thirty, with three-day stubble on his chin and jaw, he didn't look a day past twenty-two. His demeanor, on the other hand, had an old-soul quality to it. He had the ability to approach and entertain any subject, be it an ancient philosophy or random pop-culture minutia, with any person, be it a well-known political figure or a bum straight off the street.

That, of all things, was what I found the most confusing, how he could revert back and forth between different personas with such ease and without ever sounding phony or losing his characteristic charm. That was probably also why he, like his father, had found his niche in writing. It presented the perfect platform to explore and develop all those different parts within him. Personally, I found it to be just one more reason why I hated being around him. I didn't know how to interact with him and that made me terribly self-conscious. The fact that I could not engage in conversation like a normal person with someone who was clearly able to do it with everyone else made me seriously contemplate the idea that I suffered some type of social malady.

On that Monday, though, I sat with him at the Café Olé for almost an hour, the longest amount of time that I remembered spending with him as an adult without needing the presence of a third or fourth person to serve as a buffer between us. Close to fifty different people marched in and out as Lalo and I sat quietly in the corner drinking our coffees. At first, I had pulled out a manila folder from my workbag to use as a decoy. Pretending that I was reviewing paperwork had always kept me from having to talk to him. After a few minutes of fake reading and unnecessary paper shuffling, though, I realized that Lalo was really not paying attention to me or anyone else in the café anyway. Mostly he was just staring out the window. Occasionally, he would turn to look at something inside the café, but it was clear that his thoughts were elsewhere.

Just past seven o'clock, after a few more uneventful exchanges, I finally decided to head for the office. In an uncharacteristically relaxed state, I stepped over Lalo's bookbag on the floor and without realizing it caught the arm strap of the bag on my left heel. My heart dropped to my stomach as I flew forward at least thirty inches. My feet struck the floor hard at least four times and my arms circled wildly in all directions, but by some precious miracle I managed to compose myself before I spilled entirely over the Café Olé floor. Blood rushed to my face as I turned back to look at Lalo. He sat calm as ever still staring out the window toward Speedway Boulevard. He had missed my magnificently klutzy performance completely. Embarrassed yet relieved all at the same time, I crossed myself (one of the many deeply ingrained Catholic motions that still came automatic) and walked out of the café as fast as my clumsy feet would take me. I was 0 for 2.

8

Since its beginnings, coffee has been an object of great scrutiny. In the sixteenth century, it was linked to impotence and deemed by some as a threat to religious sobriety. More recently it has been investigated in connection with other health afflictions. Despite all of the negative publicity and the negative medical indications for some, it is difficult to find someone who does not drink it. For its pleasurable flavor and its stimulating effects, coffee is one beverage that few can go without.

The girls from the neighborhood started hanging around our front yard a lot more after Marcela and David moved in across the street from us. They never did anything useful while they hung out by the water fountain or propped themselves up on the white-washed boulders that marked the end of our yard. They just loitered about talking and laughing extra loud any time Alex or Lalo would come out of their house. Sometimes when they got a little anxious or desperate for attention, they would push each other around playfully and cuss out loud for no particular reason. At first I found it completely obnoxious, their invasion of my water fountain space especially. After a while, though, I began to find it somewhat entertaining. It was almost like watching a pack of wild animals carrying out their courtship rituals on *Animal Planet*. An extravagant display of the tail here, a bit of play-fighting or a blood-curdling scream there, the parallels were truly spectacular. Of course, being the irremediable observant nerd that I was, there came a point when I actually looked forward to going home and watching the girls loaf and frolic and toddle about aimlessly by the front yard. Despite the many times that I felt embarrassed for them as I watched from a distance, to the point where it became almost a normal state for the little hairs on my forearms to stand erect all the time, the spectacle was really much too amusing to be missed.

Yahdyrah Jazzmynn Perez (spelled as such, even though she oftentimes misspelled it herself by missing an 'h' here or there or substituting an 'i' for a 'y') was the leader of the pack. Although she was at least a year older than me, she had always been in my grade at school. Rumor was that she had flunked out of either third or fourth grade, perhaps both. Although I never knew for certain, the one thing that I did know was that she had always looked way older than the rest of us. Like Ramona, she towered at least a full head above most of the other kids in school and in our neighborhood. Unlike Ramona, though, she was not a pleasant sight to look at, no matter how hard she tried. She always wore tight blue jeans and brightly colored halter tops with matching shoes and hoop earrings. Her face was always buried under thick layers of turquoise-blue eye shadow, mandarin-orange blush and tacky red lipstick that went carelessly outside of her lip line making her mouth look extra big on her rather small and ant-like face. Her long, permed and bleached hair was also in pretty bad shape most of the time and, during the dry summer months especially, could have easily been considered a serious fire hazard. Even so, Yahdyrah loved to fondle and flip it from side to side before arranging it on top of her kiwi-shaped head with a plastic hair clip. Just when I thought the blaze risk had been contained, she would let her hair back down, fondle, flip and rearrange it again. The pattern would repeat itself over and over again as the afternoon progressed.

Yahdyrah's voice was always the first to be heard whenever I would walk out of my house. If Alex or Lalo were already out, usually playing basketball in their driveway, Yahdyrah's nasally voice would be twice as loud. Mocking and making fun of the other girls in her pack was always her specialty. "Nice outfit, so-and-so," she would say as she nudged whoever happened to be immediately next to her. "When did you start taking hand-me-downs from the hookers down at the Tecolote Bar?" Day after day I heard her poke fun at everything from clothes to shoes to haircuts to cars and homes and even health issues. "I love your eye shadow," she once told a girl who suffered from vitiligo and had skin discolorations throughout her knuckles, neck and eyelids. "I hear the zebra look is in these days."

The girls never countered any of Yahdyrah's backhanded compliments. Despite the nice assortment of defects (intellectual, physical and otherwise) that they could have picked from to even out the score a bit, not once did I hear them say anything to her. I was always torn between feeling angry or sorry for the girls for not having the gall to stand up to Yahdyrah. Even though sympathy usually got the best of me in the end, I still could not understand why they took her abuse like they did.

To Yahdyrah's chagrin, Alex and Lalo kept mostly to themselves. Occasionally, when the frustration of being ignored reached too high a point, one of the girls would teasingly throw one of Yahdyrah's hair clips into the boys' yard. Alex or Lalo would pick up the hair clip, hand it back to Yahdyrah and then resume the game of hoops without much more ado. They never made any effort to initiate a real conversation.

After a few weeks of failed attempts at significant contact with the boys, Yahdyrah and her clan finally gave up. They took their shove-and-curse act a few houses down the street where they had spotted fresh new meat and, for the first time in a long time, I was able to walk out of my house without hearing Yahdyrah's babble in the foreground. I was basking in the intimacy and silence of my reclaimed territory by the water fountain when another voice interrupted.

"Why aren't you with your friends down the street?" Alex stood a few feet away from me dribbling the basketball from hand to hand. Lalo waited in the driveway behind him.

"'Cause I don't want to." I had just begun to savor my newly re-acquired privacy and I didn't feel like engaging in conversation with anyone.

"Are they really your friends?" He took a few steps forward.

"Do you ever see me with them?" I turned up to look at him but was only able to make out a dark silhouette in front of the bright, setting sun in the background.

"No, not really."

"Well, there you go." I leaned back against the base of the fountain and closed my eyes. I really didn't want to be disturbed any further. I heard the basketball bounce more vigorously across the street and assumed the boys had gone back to their game. As I prepared to take in the last of the sunrays left in the afternoon, his voice struck me from above once again.

"Do you like being alone all the time?"

I opened my eyes and sat up straight. I tried to shade off some of the light with my left hand but was still unable to make out his face clearly. I could only see the outline of his tidy haircut and his broadening shoulders underneath a short-sleeved T-shirt.

"I mean, I don't think there's anything wrong with that," he added before I could respond. "I just notice that you don't usually do what all the other girls do."

"What's that? Cuss out loud for no good reason and throw lice-infested hair clips at you?" My eyes adjusted slightly to the light and I noticed a smile form on his lips. He had a nice smile.

"Well, you don't wear shoes to begin with." His smile widened. His teeth looked impeccably white next to his bronze, sunbathed skin. His nose wrinkled up a bit when he smiled, too. It was a surprisingly pleasant sight. I suddenly felt the need to come back with a smart answer, but my wit failed me terribly. I noticed his eyes glance over at my feet and, for a second, I wished the earth could swallow my thick, cracked heels. It had been almost a week since my grandmother had made one last effort to salvage them and I had done an extra good job of mangling them since then. A strange wave of self-consciousness swept over me as I sat frozen and unable to speak.

"You've got pretty toes," he said as he started jogging backward toward his house. Instinctively, I curled my toes in as far under my feet as they would go. He flashed one last smile before he took the ball from Lalo and started bouncing and shooting it haphazardly.

During the days that followed, I debated whether or not to go out into my front yard. Alex was usually outside and I didn't want him to think that I was forcing my presence on him like Yahdyrah had done. At the same time, though, I really did want to make myself present. When I did find the courage to go out, I debated whether or not I should wear shoes. If I walked out barefoot it would almost be like throwing a dirty, old hair clip at him. Things had gotten so complicated all of a sudden. I no longer enjoyed prancing around in my bare feet. Worse than that, when I showered I found myself pulling out the old pumice stones that my grandmother had given me over the years. I couldn't understand what was happening.

The first day that I decided to make my way back out was exactly one week after Ramona had run away. I waited until Alex and Lalo had finished their game of basketball and gone back inside their house. The sun had already set, leaving only light-blue and gray tones hanging in the early evening. I had picked out a pair of yellow flip-flops from the pile of mostly unused shoes thrown at the bottom of the closet that Elena and I shared. I figured they were a safe choice since they were not necessarily considered real shoes, yet they did protect my suddenly all-important heels. Of course, the fact that my toes were still visible with the flip-flops was unquestionably another big reason why I had opted to wear them.

I tiptoed my way toward the water fountain in the middle of the yard as if somehow tiptoeing on the soft, green grass would help make me less noticeable. I had just sat down on the rear side of the fountain, my back toward the street, when I heard a door close across the way. Immediately, I pulled my feet up and tucked them underneath me as if I were about to begin meditating. A funny tingling filled my stomach. In a strange state of paralysis, I stared blankly at the ground below me. If there were any ants or bugs crawling about, I didn't notice them. The sound of water trickling down the fountain also took second stage as my ears tuned in only to the sound of approaching feet. The seconds seemed suspended in midair as I waited for what seemed like an eternity. Just when I thought the anxiety building inside me was too much to handle, his voice broke through the stillness in the air.

9

Sunday, February 23, 2003

He asked me not to let anybody know that we had seen each other. I wouldn't have told anyone anyway, not even if he would have forgotten to ask. Eminem was halfway through his hypnotizing rendition of "Lose Yourself" on the Grammy Awards (his delivery flawless, his body rhythmically bopping to the beat, his right hand loosely cradling his manhood) when the doorbell rang. As usual, Mimi was spread across the entire length of my legs on the couch so it took me at least a good minute or so to move her uncooperative, eighteen-and-a-half pound body over, get up and walk over to the front door. I hadn't been expecting anybody so, figuring some of the neighborhood kids were out selling cookies or chocolates door to door, I grabbed a handful of spare change from the table in the entrance way and convinced myself that ingesting another three pounds worth of junk food that evening would not be that harmful. When I looked through the peephole, I was surprised to see an adult form underneath the dim porch light. As if it had only been yesterday since I had last seen it, Alex's silhouette on the opposite side of the door seemed oddly familiar.

Alex had been living in Phoenix for almost six years already. He had just graduated from law school and had been serving his first year as mayor of Nogales (where the people had a weakness for electing, and the city council for appointing, almost pre-pubescent and, consequently, easily manipulated public officials) when he was offered a cabinet-level position as senior adviser on Latin American policy to the governor of Arizona. Like his maternal grandfather before him, Alex was a natural on all things political. Diplomacy and social relations were an inherent part of him and, whether on a professional or personal level, you could count on his foolproof rhetoric to help him achieve whatever it was that he set his mind on.

I opened the door on impulse without giving any thought as to why Alex might be knocking at my door, nor how I would respond to whatever it was that he was there to say. It was purely a mechanical act and, quite honestly, completely unlike me. Then again, when it came to Alex, none of the things that I had ever done had been truly characteristic of me.

"Hi, Nena." His voice was soft yet confident.

"Hi." The tone in my voice came out louder and higher than I had been expecting. A wave of insecurity immediately started to sweep over me.

"Are you alone?" He leaned slightly over to look past my left shoulder into my living room and for a minute I wished more than anything that a bundle other than Mimi, preferably a one-hundred-and-seventy-five-pound bundle with strong shoulders and a masculine jawline, would have been sitting on my couch, but, alas, my pathetic reality was that I was, in fact, alone.

"Yes. What do you need, Alex?" The tone in my voice was a little more firm and balanced this time around. Enough of my stupidity. I needed to take control.

"Nothing, Nena." He seemed a little taken aback. "I was just in town and thought I'd stop by and say hello.

"Well... hello." I was determined to stay in control.

"Hello," he repeated as his all-too-familiar smile took form on his lips. Augh! I felt every single muscle in my body weaken a little and a few pennies and nickels clinked on the floor to prove it. "Can I come in for a bit?"

I made an honest-to-God good effort to come up with an excuse to say no, but still distracted by his pearly whites, his bronze skin, his slightly wrinkled nose and the unexpectedness of the whole situation, I found my wit and self-control failing me terribly once again.

Since that second time by the water fountain in Nogales, it had become clear that my usual rules of behavior did not apply whenever I was around Alex. My ingenuity and quickness with words would disappear at the first sight of him. My sharp intuition and ability to read between the lines was also quick to vanish any time that he would talk to me. Sometimes it wasn't even that I was not able to perceive a certain pretense in his words, it was just that I honestly did not care. He had the ability to sway me and, even when the air around him had a hint of falseness to it, I seemed to relish every false breath that I took.

Our encounters by the water fountain quickly became almost a daily occurrence. Even if it was only for a few minutes each day, he always found an excuse to come over and talk to me. Initially, his attempts at conversation were always school-related, like asking me whether I knew what "hypotenuse" meant. When he realized that I could regurgitate all sorts of definitions with minimal effort and that sophomore geometry did not give him the necessary edge to impress me, his approach shifted to sports. Fernando, my brother, had always been an avid sports fan and I an avid tag-along and tomboy, so when Alex tried to teach me about first downs, fumbles, interceptions, RBIs, grand slams and double dribbles, I had to pretend like I was hearing it all for the first time. I feared that if he found out that I already knew all about them, too, he might run out of topics of conversation and refuse to talk to me any more.

During the first few encounters, I also continued to struggle with the whole dilemma of whether or not I should wear shoes. Even though I had continued to pamper my feet regularly, to the point where I was wrapping them nightly in horribly uncomfortable, gel-like moisturizing socks, I missed the freedom of stepping out in my bare feet like I had always done before. When he mentioned having a thing for "pretty feet," though, my predicament was quickly resolved. From that day forth, it was flip-flops on a daily basis. No more brainstorming required. Just like that, the first in my long series of mindless decisions and perfunctory actions, all involving Alex, came to be.

As the days passed, the minutes that we spent together turned into half-hours then into full hours. Eventually, we were sitting together until it was almost dark out. That one Friday when I saw a battered Inez come out of her house to pick up her mail, it had been almost eight o'clock at night before Alex had made his way home.

Before our conversations became too lengthy, Alex had always opted to stand a few feet away from where I always sat by the water fountain. Slowly he started making himself more comfortable until he was sitting so close to me that I could feel the heat from his body radiating onto my left arm and thigh and I could smell the subtle, salty scent of his skin combined with the fresh, fabric-softener scent of his clothes. Unsuspectingly, it was that feeling of closeness and that sense of immediacy which, over the course of a few weeks, became my biggest addiction. Any movement that separated Alex and me even remotely left a longing sensation on my skin that I found almost unbearable. Similarly, and consistent with Pavlov's theory of classical conditioning, any smell that resembled his scent (Downy, Snuggle, Bounce, Comfort and Suavitel, for example) triggered an unparalleled rush throughout my entire body whether or not he was present. Apart from the coffee-in-a-coconut concoction at Doña Pilar's, I couldn't remember ever craving anything as badly as I craved for those afternoons next to Alex.

Although we became very close very quickly, neither Alex nor I ever felt the need to put a name or qualify what we had with each other. Other people, on the other hand, seemed overly concerned. Girlfriend, boyfriend, pity-friend, friend, hag and fag were only a few of the labels that rolled off of people's tongues as they struggled to define us. Doña Lupita, of course, made it all about her, or her daughter, I should say. "The boy's just using her to get close to my Clarissa," she had said even though Clarissa and I had never been friends and rarely saw each other outside of the occasional neighborhood birthday party. "I've seen him looking at Clarissa. The poor girl is getting her hopes up over nothing."

While the theories and assumptions continued to float about, Alex and I spent our time together not the least bit concerned with the newest designations and titles being thrown around to justify us. We became more comfortable with each other every day until our conversations were practically effortless. Our physical interactions were also more spontaneous each time. After a few weeks, we were playfully bending each other's fingers until our knuckles popped, gently brushing our fingertips along each other's inner forearms or comfortably leaning up against each other to watch the remarkable Nogales sunsets with such ease that it genuinely seemed as if we had known each other for ages. My life then seemed nothing short of magical. It was simple and uncomplicated, yet profound and rich with all kinds of new emotions at the same time.

I was almost fifteen years old when Alex left for college. Although a deep emptiness lingered inside me, his daily phone calls kept my skin from dissipating and my feelings of yearning from drowning me with loneliness. In the three years since we had become close, our relationship, though still not traditionally defined, continued to grow stronger. After school, Alex started meeting me at Doña Pilar's for a round of Full City roast coffee and homework. Afterward, we would walk home together and sit by the water fountain for another half-hour or so before we would finally part ways. In a weird way, it was as if Alex had become an extension of who I was. Or, more precisely, it was as if I had become an extension of who Alex was. I could easily finish off his sentences. Oftentimes, I could even start them off as well, as if our thoughts and ideas were interchangeable. Countless number of times we would be sitting together in silence and out of nowhere start talking about the exact same thing at the exact same time, down to the very same millisecond. It was as if somehow we had fused into a single unit and even the people around us started to perceive us that way.

"Where's the boy?" Doña Pilar asked the first time that I went to the café after Alex left.

"Tucson," I said, as the reality of his absence painfully hit me. "He's started college."

"Ah." Doña Pilar nodded knowingly as if coming to some sort of realization. She got up from her stool by the cash register and walked over to the coffee counter. From a shelf next to the small refrigerator where she kept the coconut shells, she pulled out a red, brown and gold bottle of Tia Maria. She poured a small amount of the coffee liqueur into two small glasses with ice then topped off one of the glasses with milk. She placed the milky blend in front of me and held the other glass up close to her face.

"Drink it one small sip at a time, *ma chérie*." She let the brown liquid barely moisten her lips. "If you try to take it in all at once, you'll end up with a terrible stomach ache. Take your time. Savor it." She relit the tip end of her Partagás Lusitanias Cuban cigar. I took a small sip from my glass. The distinctively sweet and chocolaty taste of the coffee liqueur made its way smoothly down my throat. "Everything always tastes better when you take it one small sip at a time." She continued to puff and rotate her cigar until the outer rim started to glow.

What had made Alex's departure extra hard for me to swallow was that during the last few days our interactions had become noticeably different. Every touch, whether to our hands, arms or feet, was charged with a whole new level of emotion. His skin brushing softly against my skin set off an intense jolt that traveled down my back, across my chest, into the pit of my stomach and then lodged itself in a pulsating warmth between my legs. It was such an overwhelming feeling that my knees and feet oftentimes went numb with so much sensation.

In Alex, the same reaction was a bit more obvious. He had been talking about his final baseball game in Nogales or something to that effect when I grabbed a hold of his pitching arm and gently started to run my hand up and down his golden-brown skin. It was not something new, not something that I hadn't already done before. His reaction that time, however, was completely different. First there was an unexpected silence. Although I hadn't been paying too close attention to whatever it was that he was saying, phonetically it was as if his voice had suddenly fallen off a cliff. Apparently, he had finished speaking, but an awkward inflection in his last few words made it sound as though he had only gotten halfway through his sentence. Secondly, there was a perceptible change in his breathing. Normally, his breath was calm and measured. In the sudden silence, however, it sounded distinctively heavy. The third and last sign came just a few seconds later as his khaki shorts started to rise at the crotch until a noticeable bulge protruded so far up that it formed somewhat of a tent against his zipper.

A bit confused and afraid of what was to follow, I came up with an excuse to go home early during those last few days. Once inside the safety of my house, although I had always been a morning-shower person, I began showering nightly to avoid going to bed with moist panties which had become almost a constant whenever I was with Alex.

Apart from his daily phone calls, Alex also managed to come back and visit at least once or twice every month after he left for Tucson. The new layer of tension that suddenly existed between us, though, made it difficult for us to interact with each other like we had always done before. In a way it was as if we were suddenly strangers all over again. The hand-holding, finger-popping and arm-caressing stopped altogether. We also started seeing each other only at Doña Pilar's where we were always surrounded by at least half a dozen other people. The water fountain, where our only escort had always been the distant-yet-mocking ceramic boy, quickly became a thing of the past. For three years that unsettling awkwardness lingered between us.

Then I graduated from high school and moved up to Tucson as well.

Alex was entering his senior year in college and living with Lalo in an apartment close to campus when I moved into a small house a few streets down from them on Helen Street. Both Alex and Lalo volunteered to help my dad and Fernando unload the boxes and furniture that I had brought up from Nogales. After lugging mattresses, couches, a computer desk, a TV and at least a dozen other home furnishings, Fernando and my father drove back to Nogales while Alex and Lalo helped me unpack. I focused mostly on sorting the smaller boxes in the kitchen. Alex and Lalo assembled some of the furniture in the living room. Close to nine o'clock at night, after a bit of indiscernible arguing in the living room, I heard the front door close and then saw Lalo walk past the kitchen window toward the street. He never turned to look at me. When I walked into the living room to see what was going on, Alex stood a few feet away from me next to a partially assembled bookshelf, an old familiar look perceptible in his face.

"Where's Lalo?" I asked.

"He left." Alex took a few steps forward, decreasing the distance that separated us.

"Where did he go?" A nervous rumbling started up in my stomach.

"I don't know. Home, I guess. You know how he is." A soft smile started to take shape on Alex's face as he continued to move toward me. "Don't worry about it."

I turned to look at the pieces of melamine particle board lying on the floor in an effort to break away from Alex's loaded gaze. "Are you almost done? I can fix you something to eat if you're hungry?"

I turned around and walked back into the kitchen before he could respond. Half-mindedly, I opened a box where my mom had packed some dinnerware and spices for me. I was pulling out the top bundles of newspaper-wrapped ceramic dishes and coffee mugs when the full realization of the situation hit me head-on. Alex and I were alone. We were seventy miles away from Doña Lupita's snooping glances, seventy miles away from Yahdyrah and her gang's spiteful stares, seventy miles away from Doña Pilar's Café and the water fountain, seventy miles away from everything that had ever served to buffer or curb our escalating emotions and urges. For the first time, sheltered by off-white walls and vaulted ceilings, Alex and I found ourselves completely isolated from the rest of the world.

It was not that I had never imagined or rather fantasized about that situation before. I had. A countless number of times. During the last three years, especially, I had formulated all sorts of scenes and scenarios in my head all revolving around that precise moment. Sometimes they took place inside Alex's apartment, which, in real life, I had only visited once during Lalo's nineteenth birthday party. Other times the setting was a cabin in Madera Canyon or Mt. Lemmon. Most often, however, I didn't worry about piecing together a credible or even existing backdrop. All of my creative energies went into the make-believe conversations and imaginary physical interactions instead.

Standing thick in the middle of that longed-for moment in real time, however, without the safety net of being able to rewrite dead-end conversation or redo clumsy or ineffective movements was an entirely different story. A tight knot lodged itself in the pit of my stomach as I continued to pull out newspaper bundles and small glass jars with dried cilantro, oregano, rosemary and bay leaves. I was reaching for the crushed red chili pepper when Alex's arms wrapped my waist from behind and I felt his breath brush softly against the right side of my neck. It was warm and surprisingly calm. His clearly identifiable scent, perhaps a bit more musky than usual after a full day of physical labor, triggered a frenzy of neurotransmitter synapses in my brain until every single one of my senses buzzed with anticipation. Before Alex could see the dark red powder shaking in my right hand, I dropped the glass jar back into the cardboard box and turned around to face him. Without warning, his face had taken on a more masculine, more mature shape. His jawline was strong and well defined, his cheekbones high and more pronounced than I remembered them.

We stood enveloped in a deep, meaningful silence for what seemed like an eternity, the strength of his arms still tight around my waist. His eyes, which I had initially tried to avoid, carefully studied every line and every curve of my face as his breath grew consistently heavier and deeper. When his eyes finally traced their way back up to mine, he brought his right hand gently up to my left cheek then leaned in toward me until his moist lips merged fully with mine. My soul seemed to flee right out of my body.

I remember everything that ensued after that kiss with succinct detail, as well: The moment when our impulses and instincts, no longer inhibited by anything or anyone, took over; the sensation of Alex's chin stubble scratching against my skin; the salty-sweet taste of his neck on my tongue; his arms pulling me closer toward him; his heartbeat pounding heavy against my chest; our mouths meeting time and again; our hands exploring every crease, dent and slope of our bodies.

Then the wide-angle focus fades and all of my attention converges onto a single memory. Our bodies have stopped moving away and toward each other in a synchronized rhythm. Alex rests his head on my left shoulder. His mouth finds shelter in the groove on the left side of my neck just below my ear. Then the words take form. Softly but clearly audible, Alex lets them pour out of his mouth, "I love you."

The climax of my naïveté, the biggest departure from my characteristic self: I believed him.

10

After a ripe cherry has been plucked, it is necessary to get at the seed, the core of the fruit, the coffee bean itself. This is the heart of a coffee. Unless you are able to break through the tough outer skin, you will never know the true potential and flavor of a coffee.

Thursday, March 6, 2003

I had just finished interviewing the third subject of the day, a thin and tall Polish man with pale blue eyes that looked almost white under the bright fluorescent lights in my office, when the telephone rang. It was Sasha. Normally, she would call me as soon as her plane landed safely in Las Vegas. This last time, however, she had waited three days to call. Due to the awkward circumstances under which she had left, I had not been surprised. In a sense, I had not only been expecting it but rather hoping for it as well.

Nico was the one subject that Sasha and I could not approach without giving rise to some sort of convoluted entanglement of feelings between us. We both understood that neither one of us was completely right or wrong in our positions toward him, yet our views were sometimes so different that it was impossible to grant the other total understanding and consideration. My approach typically came from a psychological perspective. It was very guarded and planned. I worried about

Nico's mental and emotional stability. I wanted him to develop into a healthy young man without carrying around any of the extra baggage that had been packed long before he was even born. Sasha was more heart-driven. She did things on impulse, always motivated by the profound love that she felt for him, but never completely aware of the full implication of her actions. For the most part, Sasha and I averted the subject of Nico entirely. When she called me that Thursday, it was clear that the old rule was being reinstated.

"I'm sorry I hadn't called. I've had early rehearsals all week and just now found the time to give you a ring. I'm so sorry, Nena." She sounded genuinely apologetic, although deep down I figured it wasn't entirely due to the fact that she hadn't called me. I think she felt sorry for having broken the old rule, for having opened the floodgate to all those emotions that she had worked so hard on suppressing, for having evoked the latent guilt that never quite left her. More importantly, I think she felt sorry for having stirred up long-buried feelings of confusion and yearning in Nico.

"Don't worry about it. I figured you were busy." I followed right along with her.

"Thank you, Nena." Her voice became small whenever she held back tears. "And thank you for driving me down to Nogales." A small pause confirmed that she was struggling to keep her emotions in check. She took a couple of deep breaths. "And for all that you always do for me, thank you." She never mentioned Nico, but by the humbled tone in her voice, I knew that he was the underlying reason for her gratitude. She knew that I would follow up with him and make sure that he was all right. We both also knew that it would be a long time before any references to Nico would be made between us.

Although Sasha was two years older than me, when it came to the mental and emotional side of things, I had always been very protective of her. After we started seeing each other at Doña Pilar's, she quickly took on the role as my defender with the Yahdyrah types and species. Even though they never gave me too much trouble to begin with (one of the upsides of being unassuming and inconspicuous), when they realized that I was a friend of Sasha's, whom we all still knew simply as Ramona, the little bit of badgering that had started up after Alex and I began seeing each other by the water fountain was reduced to a mere evil eye here and there. In return, Ramona seemed to find a safe haven and a resting place for some of her emotional burdens with me. Despite her apparent strength and outward assertive personality, there was a vulnerable side to Ramona that very few people got to see.

When we first moved in next door to her, the first thing that I noticed was the large number of girls who always seemed to flock around Ramona. Unlike Yahdyrah, though, she never resorted to yelling or using insults and bad jokes to intimidate or bully the girls into liking her. As a matter of fact, with Ramona it was quite the opposite. I remember her braiding the girls' hair and her painting their fingernails or doing their makeup if they were older. With the younger ones, she would sometimes let them sit on her lap while she told them stories or let them do her makeup until she ended up looking like a clown on crack. Even from a distance it was pretty entertaining to see.

As the afternoon moved into evening, though, Prudencio and his bottle would make their way out onto the old, rusted folding chair and the environment would change. With it, so would Ramona. The smaller girls were the first ones she sent home. Sometimes when the girls resisted being sent away, she would threaten never to let them come back and visit or let them do her makeup again. Teary-eyed the girls would mope and dawdle past my house. Occasionally, they would turn back to look at Ramona only to find her directing them farther down the street until they each made it all the way home.

The older girls would leave soon after. Unlike the younger ones, they didn't need much convincing. Prudencio's repulsive stare, his lewd gestures and inappropriate comments were enough to shoo them away. Ramona had no choice but to endure them. Since Prudencio had squirmed his way into her life, she'd had to learn to stomach many things against her will.

Prudencio first came into Ramona and Inez's life by mistake. They had been living in a two-room house on Calle Internacional in Nogales, Sonora, when he came knocking at their door. He had been looking for the unit directly behind them. It was a drop-off house used to temporarily stow baggage for people being smuggled into the United States. Although Prudencio was an American citizen and could have potentially made an honest living doing a wide range of things, his love for easy money and his general lack of regard for the human race had led him into the *pollero* business. For years he was the go-to person when it came to transporting people's belongings across the border. He charged one hundred to three hundred dollars per bag up front and then sometimes made a second profit by selling off whatever items went unclaimed. Whether the true owners ever made their way across the border or died trying, Prudencio couldn't care less. Sometimes he would rummage through their bags long before they even started their treacherous journey into the Sonoran Desert. When he found something worth anything, a good pair of sneakers for example, he would sell them off straightaway. When the owners did come looking for them some time later, he would accuse them of being ingrates for calling him a thief and then threaten to call Border Patrol on them. After his first accidental encounter with Inez, he contrived several others until his money and the possibility of a green card had ensnared Inez and convinced her of moving with him to Nogales, Arizona. Ana and Luis, Ramona's fifteen- and sixteen-year-old siblings who had also been living with them at the time, refused to go. Ramona, who was only ten, had no choice.

In her new neighborhood, Ramona stood out like a sore thumb. The language, of course, was the most marked difference, although it was only a matter of months before she was speaking fluent Spanglish. Her distinctive physical appearance, including her height, her dark caramel skin, her dark brown eyes and her long black mane, also helped place her in a category all on her own. At the end of the day, however, it was neither the language nor her physical appearance that fully set her apart. It was something far more subjective and ethereal. It was an innate ability to peak people's curiosity. Without having to utter a single word or move a single muscle, Ramona could make people naturally gravitate toward her.

At first, the kids in the neighborhood kept their distance. Ramona did not exude a friendly or welcoming demeanor at first impression. It was a trait that she had learned from her mother and one that became a core element of her defense mechanism. Trust was not a commodity that she'd had the privilege of and, as she grew older, it seemed even more foreign to her. Initially, she would come home after school and sit by her front yard to watch the kids walk by with their heavy backpacks and empty lunch bags. In her mind, she liked to visualize what each of the kids' home lives must have been like. She would picture the ceramic figurines that were probably sitting on their mantles and curio cabinets, the nightlights that were most likely plugged into their bedroom walls, the smells of boiling yams and cabbage that must have filtered out of their kitchens into their hallways, the sounds of laughter and conversation that probably governed at their dinner tables, the feel of soft cotton sheets being tucked in by a parent's gentle hands at night. She envisioned everything so vividly that the taste of *cocido* would sometimes stay with her the rest of the afternoon. Even though she had never experienced most of those things firsthand, her ability to conceptualize and piece together such detailed images in her head sometimes made her feel as if she had actually lived through them herself.

After a day or two, the kids started to slow down and dally a bit when they passed by her house. Although they didn't do or say much per se, it was evident that they were already being drawn into her magnetic field. The first to approach her was Yahdyrah. Even though she was around Ramona's age and probably just as tall, the thick layer of shiny pink goo on her lips and the bulky earrings and teased bangs that she already sported, both of which were much too big for a ten-year-old, made her look older. She stood a few feet away from Ramona and shifted her weight restlessly from one leg to the other. "Did you, like, just move here or something?" The timbre in Yahdyrah's voice was naturally irritating. It was a blend between Pee-wee Herman and Fran Drescher in *The Nanny* minus the cultish, comedic charm.

Ramona watched Yahdyrah move impatiently in front of her for a few seconds before nodding briefly. Ramona's ability to sustain an awkward silence was another major component of her defense mechanism and by far one of her strongest assets.

"What's your name?" Yahdyrah continued speaking unnecessarily loud. Before Ramona could respond, Yahdyrah turned around and yelled something back at one of the girls who was waiting for her across the street. When she turned back to face Ramona, she asked another question without waiting for Ramona's response to the first. "Anyways, are you, like, related to Prudencio?"

Ramona did not respond, that time by her own choice. Instead, she got up from her chair and looked fixedly at

Yahdyrah. She did not say anything. She only looked. She noticed tiny beads of perspiration glistening across the length of Yahdyrah's upper lip. Her nostrils were flared. Ramona continued looking. Yahdyrah's left eye was slightly smaller than her right and a subtle tightness in her chin formed a patch of dimples along the lower half of her face. Ramona looked on a bit longer. Yahdyrah's lower lip was starting to tremble. At the sight of that, Ramona turned around and walked back into her house, a deep pain already filling her chest. She couldn't stand the sight of distress in others. It would have been much easier if Yahdyrah's response had been more callous, if she would have been overtly confrontational instead, perhaps even downright cruel. Ramona could handle that. That was what she knew.

Instead, Yahdyrah had found herself at a loss for words. Even as she walked back to her awaiting pack across the street, she could not fully make sense of what had just transpired between her and the new girl. For the first time, Yahdyrah kept her mouth shut the rest of the way home. It was also the first and last time that she ever questioned Ramona about anything again.

Over time, Ramona slowly started to lower her guard until the kids felt comfortable enough to come over and hang out at her house. At first it was only the girls. By the time Ramona turned twelve and thirteen, however, the boys had started coming around, too. Even though at first glance it appeared as though Ramona was being purposely flirtatious, in time the kids realized that her flowing glances and effortlessly suave walk were an intrinsic part of her and that in reality she was more motherly than anything else, even with the boys. They also noticed, however, that on certain days Ramona showed a detachment and a coldness toward everyone that went entirely against her usual self. Unfortunately, as she grew older, that other self became more and more prevalent. By the time she turned fourteen, her usual self, the one the kids in the neighborhood had initially grown to like, had almost completely disappeared. For the most part, she was stuck in that unfeeling and distant persona. Eventually, however, that persona gave rise to yet another part of her self. From the most intricate depths of a wounded soul and a desperate defense mechanism, a whole new Ramona emerged. It was the Ramona that I remembered seeing gyrating atop an old folding chair on her front porch, an overly sexualized young girl with an apparent boldness and resiliency that, in fact, only veiled a broken and fragile soul underneath.

11

Green coffee beans are only seeds of potential flavor. Roasting is required to sculpt and enhance the flavors locked inside. The degree of heat that is applied to a particular coffee during roasting is always relative to the nature of that coffee. A soft and fragile coffee bean can only take a small amount of heat before it reaches its maximum flavor potential. A higher-grown and, therefore, harder coffee bean, on the other hand, can withstand much higher temperatures. While others start to burn or char, these just begin to manifest their wonderfully unique and complex flavors.

Before the night of the Grammy Awards, the last time that Alex and I had spoken had been April 1, 1997. It was April Fools' Day, a Tuesday. I was still studying in Tucson and he was halfway through his term as mayor of Nogales. Although his work agenda and my school schedule did not allow for us to see much of each other during those days, we did talk on the phone regularly. When he was summoned by the governor, he called to tell me the news.

"This is a great opportunity for me, Nena. It opens all kinds of doors." He sounded calm and collected, but I could sense the excitement lingering underneath. His voice became unusually deep and his rhythm very carefully paced whenever he was trying to keep his emotions from manifesting. It was almost robotic.

"That's wonderful, Alex. Congratulations!" My excitement was much more transparent. "We should celebrate," I added. "Something small and intimate. Just you and me." Subconsciously, I had turned his "me" into "us" in my head and, by extension, felt entitled to include myself in the festivities.

"Um, sure… " There was a small pause. I could hear a man's voice talking to him in the background. "Listen, Nena, I have to go. I'll give you a call once I know how all of this is going to play itself out. You know, the transition and everything."

"Of course." I felt the excitement inside me slowly start to give way to a bit of awkwardness, then embarrassment and finally full-blown regret. "Don't worry about it," I recoiled. "We'll talk later."

With Alex it had always been a very delicate balance trying to maintain a presence in his life without feeling like I was turning into a Yahdyrah Jazzmynn Perez. I cringed at the thought of ever becoming an imposition on him and so I had always been very careful not to come off as needy or dependent. The paradox of my relationship with him, however, was that he seemed to appreciate my independence when it came to the physical side of things (opening doors and pulling back chairs for myself, for example, or spending weeks at a time alone without seeing him), but when it came to the intellectual or thinking side of things, I noticed my autonomy oftentimes made him rather uncomfortable.

I had noticed it even back in our adolescent years when we started seeing each other at Doña Pilar's. Anytime I would voice my opinion on anything, Ronald Reagan or the first generation of tragic Bushes in the White House for example, he would curl the left side of his lips into a half-smile, which looked more like a smirk than anything else, and I would know that he wasn't entirely pleased. If there were other people present, Ramona, Beatriz or Doña Pilar for example, his irritation would become even more obvious. His half-smile would slowly even out and then flatline completely. At first, I began choosing the comments that I felt were worth the aggravation of watching Alex sulk for ten to fifteen minutes at a time. Eventually, though, I simply opted for keeping my opinions to myself. Just like that, another characteristic flavor became muted whenever I was around him.

After he left for Phoenix, Alex became the in-vogue topic of conversation throughout the entire city of Nogales. There wasn't a single front-page article in the local newspaper where he was not mentioned at least a half-dozen times. At first it was a welcomed change from the usual articles on drug trafficking, illegal immigrants and other small-town gossip that rarely did anything to inform, educate or stimulate the public in any beneficial way. After a full month of unrestrained glorification, though, the news quickly grew old.

The first time that I went to Doña Pilar's Café after Alex's appointment, I was surprised to hear how loud the buzz had become. Short snippets of interviews Alex had given over the past weeks were being played and replayed over and over again on the local radio station. The chatter at the tables also kept taking the form of his name: "Alex Piercy this" and "Alex Piercy that." Even Doña Lupita, who had long-since learned to dislike Alex for not having fallen madly in love with Clarissa, appeared on local television praising him and calling herself not only his neighbor but a close aunt. People built him up until they were talking about someone I barely recognized. There was a semblance of truth weaved into it all, but for the most part, the stories were highly exaggerated. As they made their way from mouth to mouth, they kept getting more embroidered and embellished until Alex was practically living in the White House. And all that time I just waited. While an entire town gushed and burbled over the new local luminary, I waited for Alex's call.

The second time around it wasn't just in the Nogales newspaper. It was splattered across several Sunday papers throughout Arizona. Within two months, Alex had been promoted once again. He was dressed in a full tuxedo, shaking the governor's hand. The headline: *Piercy Named Executive Director of Arizona-Mexico Commission*. The article was dated June 1, 1997, exactly sixty days after Alex and I had last spoken. The subheading: *Phoenix, AZ - A formal reception with over 300 attendants was held Saturday night in honor of Alex Piercy, 26, who has just been named Executive Director of the Arizona-Mexico Commission by Governor Ruth Thompson.*

The article itself was quite extensive. It went on and on about his many achievements at twenty-six and then gave an excessively detailed account of all the high-profile people who had attended. Mostly they were political figures with whom I was not familiar. Then there were Charles Barkley and Alice Cooper. For a minute, the picture of Charles and an eyeliner-free Alice made the knot in the pit of my stomach loosen up a bit. Recognizing them made me think that perhaps I was not entirely out of the loop. When I turned the page, however, the continued photo spread of the lavish reception made my gut clench up painfully once again. Smack-center on the second page was another photograph of Alex. That time he stood next to a tall and glamorous blonde. Normally, his characteristically smooth smile would have been the first thing that I noticed. As I stared at the creased image in the middle of the paper, however, it was the woman leaning in toward him and Alex's left arm cradling her waist that jumped off the page. The caption: *Alex Piercy accompanied by fiancée, Emma Matthews, daughter of Senator Joseph Matthews.*

I read and re-read the caption at least five times, but my brain could not fully register the words. No matter how hard I tried, the morphemes printed on the page made no sense to me. It was as if all reason had suddenly escaped me, as if my entire body had entered a strange state of semi-consciousness. Even as I stood in the middle of my kitchen with the newspaper firmly in hand, my body felt hollow. It was like my soul had inadvertently checked out and only an overwhelming numbness reigned throughout.

I don't recall exactly how long the numbness lasted. A few seconds or twenty minutes felt all the same to me. I do recall, however, the moment when the last thread finally gave out underneath me. In that surreal stillness I remember feeling it snap. Then, with the force of a tidal wave, all emotion gushed back into my veins at once, the pressure violently tearing through each and every one of the senses. While a tattered safety net dangled in the growing distance above me, I took the arduous plunge into heartbreak.

The hardest part by far was the helplessness, the realization that little could be done to change things or thwart the sudden upsurge of emotions. It penetrated through to the very core of my being, scorching and blistering the inner linings of my soul. For someone hell-bent on finding the logic in things and acting based on that logic, not being able to find it was twice as agonizing as the betrayal itself. It was like being stripped of all primary armor. Common sense no longer applied and the usual tactics of rationalization brought no comfort. Life seemed broken in two and neither part felt wholly mine. The rose-tinted and sheltered part behind me only made me feel foolish and naïve. The darker, harsher version of life that lay ahead seemed much too bleak and bitter. It was like sinking deeper into an ever-expanding rift and not knowing which side to grasp onto for safety.

Unlike Ramona and Inez, who had been initiated into the world of heartache and sorrow very early on, I never knew what it was like to be brokenhearted as a young girl. Deceit and betrayal were two hands that I had never been dealt before and although I was grateful, of course, I had always been much more skeptical than anything else. In my obsessive search for balance, I had always wondered why my life seemed so much simpler and uncomplicated, why my position seemed so privileged in comparison to others. As a result, an unnerving feeling had always simmered deep inside me, singeing and picking at an ever-growing scab of uncertainty. Although I had always tried to prepare myself mentally for my turn at hardship, always gravitating toward those who had already lived and survived it, no amount of third-person experiences could have ever prepared me fully. When life saw to it that scores were evened out a bit, I realized just how naïve I had truly been. No matter how many times I had sung about it in songs, seen it in movies or helped chase it away from friends, at twenty-two, heartbreak was still a concept that was completely foreign to me. None of the lyrics that I had sung or lines that I had heard or sound advice that I had given others seemed either relevant or helpful when it was me who stood broken, my heart shattered in pieces.

I stood rigid next to the screaming kettle on the stove for at least two more minutes before the numbness finally faded completely and the anguish fully took over. A clenching tightness took hold of my chest and pressed heavily against my diaphragm until I was barely able to breathe. Then my head began spinning and an uncontrollable churning started up in my stomach. Finally, a throbbing heat slowly started to make its way up from my stomach, through my esophagus, into my chest and, just before it found its way up past my throat, I dropped the newspaper to the floor and rushed to the bathroom. I was still hugging the toilet fifteen minutes later when the telephone rang.

12

For a split second I thought that it might be Alex calling to explain the misunderstanding, how it had been a careless typo, how he had been confused with someone else, how the photo reporter had obtained inaccurate information, how the entire newspaper staff and editors had failed to verify the facts, how there was really a simple and sensible explanation that could mend my torn world back into one piece. A fleeting sense of hope filled my heart as I forced my body off of the floor in the bathroom and made my way into the bedroom toward the cordless telephone.

"Hello?" My voice was raspy and my throat stung from the empty-stomach acids that had just made their way out of my body.

"Hi, Nena," Lalo responded on the other end. "Were you sleeping?"

The last thing that I needed was Lalo's heckling. I seriously contemplated putting the handset back on the charger but figured it would only give him that much more pleasure to see me defeated, unable to withstand his not-so-meaningless banter. I assumed he was calling because he figured that I had already read the newspaper. Still I tried not to let on. "Yes," I responded curtly. "I was just about to get up."

He was quiet for a few seconds and then caught me off guard. "Listen, I had a writing workshop that just got canceled today and I was wondering if you weren't too busy, maybe we could have lunch or catch a movie or something."

I must have stayed quiet longer than I realized because the next thing that I heard was Lalo's voice asking if I was still there. "No, I mean, yes," I stumbled with my words. "I mean no, I didn't go anywhere and, yes, I'm still here." A nervous rumble started up in my already weak stomach as I desperately tried to dissect his invitation. After all, there had to be an underlying motive. Surely he wanted to rub in Alex's treachery, highlight my idiocy for not having seen the signs, for having trusted Alex blindly. But why make it a lunch date? Why not begin the torture straightaway? I tried putting my good sense back to work, but no matter how hard I tried I just couldn't figure it out fast enough. My brain was not yet fully functional.

"You don't have to if you don't want to, Nena." He sounded a little hurt, which only threw me off further.

"No, that's fine, Lalo. I'm not busy. We can grab something to eat." I could hardly believe the words as they floated out of my mouth. I was voluntarily accepting to go to lunch with Lalo. Alone. He agreed to pick me up at 1:30. As if on cue, I hung up the phone and the churning in my stomach started up again.

Normally, I spent most Sundays with Sasha. It was her last year working at the Tecolote Bar and if she wasn't able to drive up to Tucson, then I would make the hour-long drive down to Nogales. Every now and then, if he wasn't too consumed by work (or apparently conquering other politicians' daughters' hearts), Alex would join us. A couple of times Lalo came along, too, although most of the time it was as if he really wasn't there. I never quite knew if it was me or Sasha or Alex or perhaps some mix-and-match combination of the three of us that bothered Lalo so, but every time that the four of us were together, he would shut down. His conversations were scarce and his usual penetrating looks were reduced to a few passing glances here and there. And he never looked at Sasha. While everyone else ogled Sasha at the first opportunity (yes, Alex included), Lalo never turned to look at her.

Back in Nogales, I had always figured that Lalo had a thing for Sasha, whom he always insisted on calling Ramona. Not just a silly crush like most of the other boys, but something more serious. They had always been in the same grade in school and, after Ramona dropped out halfway through her freshman year in high school, there was a noticeable change in Lalo. He had never been one to flock around her. As a matter of fact, he had always been much more of a loner. After Ramona ran away from home, though, he seemed to submerge himself deeper into his voluntary solitude. His basketball games with Alex came to an abrupt halt and I rarely saw him interact with anyone else. Every now and then, when I came across him at Doña Pilar's Café, he would be sitting alone at the same table where his father always sat. He was always scribbling onto a faded brown leather journal. If I was with Ramona or Alex, he would ignore us entirely. If I was alone, though, I would oftentimes find him looking over in my direction by the front counter. Usually, I would glance past him quickly and pretend like I hadn't noticed him looking. Sometimes, even without having to turn around, I could sense his eyes studying me intently. As usual, not knowing exactly what was going through his mind made me terribly self-conscious. So in an attempt to break away from his line of sight, I started helping Doña Pilar roast coffee in the back room whenever he was there. By the time I made my way back out, my curly hair more rebellious than usual from the sweat and heat of the roasting room, Lalo would already be gone. Throughout most of our years in Nogales, and Tucson for that matter, that was the closest we came to interacting with each other on a one-on-one basis.

Soon after I hung up the phone with Lalo, I quickly started to regret having accepted his invitation. My heart felt unusually heavy as it was. I was still trying to sort through the muddle of emotions that the newspaper had triggered and I just didn't have the energy or the will to deal with Lalo's cynicism and irony on top of it all, especially not alone. Several times I picked up the phone to call and cancel on him, but before I could finish dialing his number, I would somehow convince myself that it would only be like admitting defeat. Besides, he had sounded different. The tone in his voice had been softer, warmer even. True, it could have been a disguise for his deeper, more sinister intentions, but how could I be sure? My good judgment had taken a serious blow that morning and I just couldn't think straight.

Finally, when I realized that I couldn't come up with a good enough excuse or, more truthfully, that I just didn't have the nerve to cancel on him, my weak escape was to invite Sasha along with us instead.

Lalo pulled into the driveway in his ramshackle '82 Chevy S10 at exactly 1:30. The pickup truck, which he had purchased for twelve hundred dollars just before moving up to Tucson, was exactly what you would have expected Lalo to be driving. It was mid-size and had originally been all white with silver trim. As he drove closer, though, you could see that the white was now more of a burnt beige and only served as an opaque background for at least twelve other colors, each representing a different car, wall or lamppost that had been, at one point, crashed into by the old clunker. Similarly, what had once been silver now looked a dark rusty brown. The kicker was that Lalo had purchased the truck in those conditions already. Minus a few scratches here and there, the truck had looked just as beaten up when Lalo had decided to buy it almost six years back.

Sasha had arrived at my house about an hour before Lalo. After ridding my body of the last bit of liquids left in my stomach that morning, I had curled up on the cold floor next to the toilet and replayed the last conversation that Alex and I'd had at least ten different times in my head. No matter how many times I went over the details, though, I just couldn't pinpoint any real indication for anything as extreme as what the newspaper was claiming. Not even the robotic tone in his voice or the awkwardness that I had felt after hanging up with him had tipped me off even slightly. For convenience sake, perhaps, I had chosen to believe that he was really just too busy with work to call me. And, of course, I would have never dared bother him with a call of my own. Plus, now there was the gratuitous issue of Lalo's random invitation. For an ordinary Sunday and an even more ordinary person with an astoundingly ordinary life, things seemed suddenly much too complicated. I lay in my bathroom in a total state of shock for almost an hour before the long overdue cry fest finally started. When Sasha arrived, I had just gotten out of the shower yet I still looked a mess. Quickly she pulled out her cosmetics bag from her purse, blotted all the shininess away and applied a little more makeup than usual around my eyes to disguise the red puffiness. On my lips, which looked more like Lisa Rinna's, she went easy on the lip liner and applied only a little bit of clear lip gloss instead.

As usual, Sasha had parked her '88 silver Nova in the back side of the house so when she opened the front door for Lalo, I immediately noticed the surprise in his face. The discomfort was pretty obvious as well and, for a moment, I couldn't help but feel sorry for him. It was as if my own vulnerability made me more sensitive to the vulnerabilities of others, even Lalo's. Still he walked in and greeted us both with a brief, one-handed hug and a cheek-to-cheek kiss. It was his classic ability to move through an awkward social situation with the coolest and most natural of composures. Still, while Sasha made one last run to the bathroom, I felt compelled to give him an explanation.

"I forgot she was coming up for the day," I lied. "I hope it doesn't bother you if she joins us."

His green eyes looked fixedly at me like they always did whenever we were alone, but there was definitely a softer feel to them. "That's fine, Nena." He walked up a little bit closer than usual, his eyes studying mine. My stomach started to do all kinds of funny flips. "I can still see you behind all that makeup, you know." His voice was so soft that it was almost a whisper, as if he were talking to himself.

"Excuse me?" I pretended not to follow. Before he had the chance to repeat his words and open the way for a conversation that I was not yet ready to have, Sasha came back into the living room and inadvertently saved me once again.

When we walked outside, I noticed one more thing about Lalo's multihued Chevy S10. It only seated two. A third person would either have to ride in the back or squeeze into the empty space between the driver and passenger seats. I struggled to come up with a good excuse to convince Sasha into the middle position, but consistent with all my other intellectual attempts of the day, I failed horribly. The next thing I knew I was sitting atop a roadside emergency kit, pressed tightly against Lalo to my left and Sasha to my right, the stick shift and, consequently, Lalo's right hand moving in circles between my knees. I tried hard to lean more toward Sasha's side, but after only a few blocks, my left buttock and thigh muscles were already cramping. When Lalo announced that we were driving up to Bisbee, which was an hour and thirty minutes east of Tucson, I finally gave up and released every muscle and every bias in my body.

Café

When I was a kid, I had often taken spur-of-the-moment road trips with my family. It was something we had all enjoyed. Sometimes we didn't really know exactly where we were heading. We would just pack our bags and hit the road. It had been a liberating feeling. No one to dictate where we could or couldn't go. We would drive for hours at a time listening to my parents' music compilations with Stevie Wonder, Juan Gabriel, Barry Manilow, José José, Whitney Houston, Diego Verdaguer, Fleetwood Mac, Luis Miguel and even a little Madonna all on the same cassette tape. Singing our hearts out, we would take in the varied Arizona scenery. Within half an hour we would come across tall, red rock mountains then hit dense patches of Fremont cottonwood and Gooding willow trees then seamlessly sail back into endless yellow sand speckled with hundred-year-old saguaros, mesquite trees and Sacaton grass. Every now and then we would pull off the main road for a bathroom break or to eat at one of the local restaurants. When darkness fell, we would find the closest motel to sleep in, but early the next morning, coffee in hand, we would be off again. Fixing flats and finding our way back into civilization when we accidentally took a wrong turn became like second nature to us. It was adventure at its best.

Driving up to Bisbee that Sunday brought back the memory of those days and it filled me with an unexplainable sense of peace. When we drove through Mule Pass Tunnel, I even went so far as to reach across Lalo to honk the entire way through the dimly lit tunnel. It was something my parents had always done. Interestingly, both Lalo and Sasha seemed to humor me and even looked a bit amused themselves. For a second, the void in the center of my heart seemed momentarily to vanish. As we drove out of the tunnel, the picturesque town of Old Bisbee came into sight.

Unlike the more modern subdivisions in the bigger city of Bisbee, the historic downtown area of Old Bisbee still had the authentic feel of the old Southwest. Despite its slightly more polished look, a result of its rebirth from an ailing mining town to an artist colony, the original Victorian-style architecture, which still prevailed throughout, and the European-like hilly terrain gave the quaint little town an Old-World feeling. Lalo invited us to lunch at the Winchester Restaurant inside the Copper Queen Hotel. The Copper Queen, which was best known for its restless spirits and other-worldly phenomena, had always intrigued me as a child. I loved hearing the stories about a tall, older gentleman who was said to leave behind the aroma of a good cigar, or the accounts of a small boy who reportedly moved objects in the guestrooms and was oftentimes heard giggling, crying or running through the hallways. Mostly, though, I was always fascinated by the stories of a dark, figureless young woman who roamed the saloon, the west wings of the second and third floors and especially room 318. She was said to have been a female in her early thirties by the name of Julia Lowell. The stories claimed that Julia had been a lady of the night who had used the rooms at the hotel to meet with her clients. It was believed that when she confessed her love to one of her clients, his rejection resulted in her taking her own life inside room 318. Since then, there had been reports of a female voice whispering into men's ears as they slept.

A few times my parents, Fernando, Elena and I intentionally stayed in room 318, the Julia Lowell Room. With a mixture of fear and excitement I had always looked forward to witnessing some sort of supernatural activity, windows and doors opening and closing on their own, lights flickering, doorknobs jiggling or locking themselves, perhaps even a cold spot here or there. I longed for the opportunity to write my own anecdote in the "Copper Queen Encounters" scrapbook that sat on the front desk in the administration, but to my great disappointment, nothing worth writing ever happened.

When I walked into the turn-of-the-century-looking lobby that Sunday, I felt that old familiar feeling of excitement again. The unsettling ball of nerves that was usually stuck in the pit of my stomach, however, was gone. Instead, a strange feeling of ease came upon me, a weird sense of belonging. Inside the restaurant, we sat at a table by a corner window. Lalo ordered the Tiger shrimp pan-seared with sun-dried tomatoes, kalamata olives, artichokes and feta cheese. Sasha and I both ordered the fettuccine with a fresh vegetable medley sautéed in oil and garlic.

Conversation was scarce, but the silence, complimented by the red wine and the soft murmur of the guests around us, seemed to be something we all appreciated.

After lunch we took a walk through the mostly uphill, narrow streets of Old Bisbee. The air was surprisingly cool for an early June afternoon. Sasha, as usual, walked slightly ahead of us, a natural by-product of her endlessly long legs. Lalo and I walked mostly side by side a few steps behind her. When the sidewalk became so narrow that we couldn't both fit without brushing up against each other, I would slow down my pace to give him a slight advantage a step or two ahead of me. Casually, he would slow down and let me catch up to him again. As I took in the fresh air, I could almost taste the oldness of the place. It was as if time had suddenly stopped there about a hundred years back. As we made our way past the park and the museum, past the art deco courthouse and the brewery and stock exchange, that profound feeling of peace that had begun during the drive up, continued to thrive inside me. When we reached the top end of the street, my heart was pounding heavily inside my chest and goose bumps crawled up and down my spine yet a deep serenity still governed within me. When I turned to look at Lalo, I noticed his face was also flush and his breathing heavy. His eyes on me, however, were as gentle as I had ever seen them.

On our way back down, trailing at least twenty steps behind Sasha, we walked strictly side by side. A few times, when the sidewalk tapered, Lalo would lift his left arm slightly and place his hand softly on my lower back as if to guide me through in front of him. When we finally reached the bottom, an overwhelming buzz traveled throughout my entire body. Sasha waited on one of the park benches. When we came up to her, I immediately noticed the expression on her face as she looked at me. It was that subtle, knowing smile that always appeared whenever she came upon some sort of realization before I did. The thing was that this time I knew what she was thinking and I also knew that she was wrong. Yes, Lalo and I were strangely getting along. And, yes, I suddenly wasn't feeling or looking half as shitty as I had earlier in the day. But that was it. There was nothing else going on between Lalo and me. Still, it took no more than two seconds for Sasha to innocently kill my buzz completely. "Come on, lovebirds, we're gonna miss the movie."

I didn't dare respond or even acknowledge her choice of words. Instead, I sped up my pace until both Sasha and Lalo lagged far behind me.

The old movie theater in Bisbee had recently re-opened and only played old, classic films. That weekend it was playing all '80s movies and *Back to the Future*, one of my all-time favorites, was playing at 5:00 p.m. I asked for two tickets at the booth, but before I could hand the teller my twelve bucks, Lalo bumped me over and paid for all three of our tickets.

"I invited you, remember?" He sounded a little annoyed, but again, more hurt than anything else.

"But I'm the one who invited Sasha, you shouldn't have to pay for her." I could feel his eyes on me, but like a stubborn five-year-old, I didn't turn to look at him anymore.

"I know. You couldn't stand the thought of being alone with me, could you?"

The peace and serenity that had reigned inside me just a few minutes back slowly started to seep out of my system. I had no idea how to respond to his unquestionably accurate accusation.

"Don't worry about it," he interjected before I was forced to fabricate some phony excuse. "I didn't think you would even come at all. I was expecting you to call and cancel, but I guess inviting Sasha is more like you." He handed me my ticket and then turned around and walked into the theater with Sasha. I stood next to the ticket booth feeling completely exposed and outed.

Inside I made it a point not to sit in the middle. I sat next to Sasha, two seats away from Lalo. Throughout the movie, which I was hardly able to follow, I discreetly glanced over at him a few times, but every time he was looking straight ahead at the wide screen. Normally, I would have been delighted to have Marty and Doc distract him so, but that time it was different. I felt a little sad, disappointed even, to see how easily he could ignore me. The worst part was that I couldn't figure out why I was so upset. After all, he wasn't all that important to me. If anything, I should have still been worrying and hurting for Alex. He was the one who mattered. I absentmindedly watched George McFly knock Biff out with a left hook outside the *Enchantment Under the Sea Dance* when the realization suddenly hit me: I hadn't thought about Alex in at least four hours.

Before we took the drive back home, I made one last trip to the bathroom inside the Copper Queen Hotel. Past the saloon, I walked into the ladies' room and took the first stall on the left. While I sat quietly relieving myself, the bathroom door swung open again and I heard someone walk into the stall next to me. I was listening to the fading trickle of my pee when a soft sobbing sound started to make its way across the thin sheetrock partition. For a minute it sounded just like Sasha. When I called out her name, though, the sobbing became muffled and then died down completely. In the sudden silence, I felt a cold rush sweep over me and a patch of goose bumps formed on my exposed thighs. By the time I stepped out to wash my hands, the bathroom door was swinging shut again and, although I poked my head out into the hallway to see if Sasha had just left, I was not able to see anyone. When I walked past the saloon on my way out, the bartender looked at me a bit perplexed.

"Is something wrong?" I asked. His expression was somewhat hesitant as he shook his head from side to side. "Did a tall woman with dark, long hair just walk by here?" I continued questioning him. Again he shook his head, that time a bit more vigorously. I walked back into the lobby and through the front door window I saw Lalo and Sasha waiting for me inside the pickup truck. Sasha sat immediately next to Lalo on top of the roadside emergency kit that I had sat on during our drive up. The void in my heart slowly started to take shape again. Before making my way out, I walked over to the front desk, grabbed a blue pen from the counter, shuffled through the ragged pages in the scrapbook and wrote:

Sunday, June 1, 1997

Today, Bisbee's infamous lady of the night, Julia Lowell, and I both knew what it is like to be brokenhearted. – Ximena

I didn't speak a single word throughout the entire drive home. Lalo and Sasha only exchanged a few words but, for the most part, Sasha slept her way back to Tucson. She took turns leaning her head comfortably against my left shoulder and Lalo's right one and, for a minute, I truly envied her ability to just be, her capacity to do things without having to scrutinize every last detail, every last one of her movements. At one point, I saw Lalo rest his shifting hand on her left knee and an unexpected, piercing pain turned in my stomach. When he dropped us off at my house, he bid us a generalized "good night" and then drove off without once turning to look at me. Again, the worst part was that my eyes had actually been waiting to meet his. Sasha made one last run to the bathroom, gave me one last hug and then got into her car and drove back to Nogales. I stood alone in the middle of my driveway watching the Nova's rear lights turn into red specks in the horizon and then disappear completely into the starless desert night. Once inside my house, I didn't bother with clothes or shoes or the ton of makeup that was still smeared around my eyes. I just crawled into my bed, my soul weighing heavier than ever on me, and let myself plummet into month after month of the rawest of heartaches.

13

There are two major species of coffee grown in the world: Coffea robusta and Coffea arabica. Robusta, which is grown down slope, generally has a dirtier and harsher flavor. It also has a higher yield per plant and, therefore, a lower cost of production, which makes it an institutional favorite.

Arabica, on the other hand, is grown in higher elevations and is the origin of all specialty coffees throughout the world. Specialty coffees are distinguished primarily by the quality of their raw material and also by the degree of attention that is paid to their processing. In general, arabica has a longer, slower growth cycle but also delivers a far more intense flavor in the cup. Because of its harder nature, an arabica can also undergo the darkest of roasts without losing its integrity.

Friday, May 26, 1989

It was the last day of school in eighth grade and I woke up in an especially good mood. Although I had always been a good student, always ranking in the top five in my class, I never considered myself to be a bona fide school junkie. As a matter of fact, even though I took some pleasure in knowing that I could do well in most subjects, I loved days off more than anything else. In all honesty, I never considered myself to be school smart, not like Omar Ontiveros or Elizabeth Ochoa, who were legitimate *Good-Will-Hunting*-type geniuses. They were always the ones to point out Mr. Gonzalez's clumsy mistakes in algebra or correct Ms. Taylor's flubbed theories in natural science. I was more of a hard worker, an overachiever of sorts. At first it was due to the language barrier. I had spoken Spanish only until I was four or five years old so in order to grasp even part of the class material, I had to kick it into high gear early on and learn English first. Eventually, it just became a deep-rooted part of me, doing a little more, studying a bit longer than the average student. It was because of that self-imposed double workload that school usually represented for me that I so desperately looked forward to the three-month break every summer.

On Thursday night, I had taken a white undershirt from my dad's dresser drawer and a metallic-gold marker from my mom's craft supplies. I had stuffed them both into my otherwise empty backpack and looked forward to the unconventional school day that followed. The last day of school was traditionally not about learning or accomplishing any real tasks. The whole point was to show up at school, sign people's yearbooks and shirts, have them write their stock wishes on your yearbook and shirt, and then head back out only two hours later. The messages were always the same, too.

Nena,

You seem like a cool person. Have a great summer and good luck with the boys!

Your friend,

Hilda

or

Nena,

It was great getting to know you this year. Don't ever change. See you next year!

> *Always,*
>
> *Yvette*

For the most part, the boys didn't bother with the corny and tired one-liners. Unlike Hilda Castro and Yvette Robinson, they put minimal effort and only signed their names: *James Soto, Conor Herrera, Juan Osborne, Luis Valenzuela, Sean Jackson*, etcetera, etcetera.

On the last day of school in junior high, it had also become tradition to head over to City Hall after the early release. There, everyone would spray each other down with can after can of shaving foam for no particular reason. Although I had mentally psyched myself up for the Fruit of the Loom sign-off (I had never been naturally inclined toward tradition and had, therefore, learned to rely on an auto pep talk every now and then), the spray-down had been too big of a stretch for me so I hadn't bothered to make off with one of my dad's Edge shaving foams. I figured that going unarmed would save me all the trouble and the mess, but when school let out at ten o'clock sharp, the first thing that I encountered was J.J. Rodriguez squirting thick, white fluff onto my face and head. Before I could react or say anything, he raced off and started squirting a few other kids who were standing in the hallway by the lockers. Immediately, I felt the ringlets start to tighten up on my head. Although I had never been one to obsess much about my hairdo (an inevitable result of growing up with naturally unmanageable hair), at that very moment, as I felt my hair shrink up with the sticky, white lather, I couldn't help but feel annoyed and self-conscious.

At one point during the morning, influenced by the intoxicating end-of-school excitement that lingered in the air, I had actually contemplated following the crowd downtown toward City Hall. After the spray-down, the kids would throw each other into the water fountains in the front park and then hang out until either the city employees shooed them away or their clothes dried stiff and smeared with the watered-down metallic ink that had just a few hours earlier read meaningless wishes for the future. As I rethought walking home with sticky hair, stiff shorts and, consequently, chafed inner thighs, the idea no longer seemed very appealing. While my hormone-infused peers swarmed toward City Hall, I took the shortcut to Doña Pilar's Café instead.

As usual, the café was bustling when I walked in. At least twenty people were getting their mid-morning fix as Beatriz trailed around the small tables carrying mug after mug of hot coffee. The scent of fresh ground coffee and sweet Mexican pastries filled every corner in the café. It was enough to get my heart pumping and my mind off of the dry gunk on my face and hair. I walked all the way back into the room where Doña Pilar was already roasting.

"*Bon jour*, my love." Doña Pilar's facial expression was contagiously serene despite the deafening sound of the huge contraption in front of her.

"Good morning."

"Come, come." She gestured with her left hand as she signaled the cooling tray with her right one. "Spread the beans out nice and evenly, *querida*." She opened the front door on the roasting machine and left me to scoop out the hot, dark brown, shiny coffee beans. She walked over to the water faucet in the corner and put a white hand towel under the running water. I was scooping out the last of the beans when I saw her wring out the towel and walk back slowly to where I stood. Although Doña Pilar was only 54 at the time and still looked strong, her step had a bit of a side to side toddle to it which made it clear that the many years of hard physical labor that she had put into the plantation had undoubtedly taken a toll on her body. Her knees and hips were clearly not what they had been even a few years back. When she made it all the way back to where I still stood, without saying a word, she started wiping the accumulated dried lather off of my forehead and hairline. The warm, moist towel felt good on my otherwise stiff face. For a minute I felt a compulsion to explain to her what had happened, how J.J. Rodriguez had piled it on even though I had been unarmed, how he had dragged me into a foolish tradition without my consent. As she continued wiping away quietly, however, I realized that it really wasn't necessary. After she finished cleaning off most of my face, she placed her right hand gently on my left cheek. A subtle tenderness emanated right through her callused skin. "You girls are a rare batch of seeds, *bonita*." She patted my cheek softly a few times. "True specialty coffees." She looked at me thoughtfully for a few more seconds and then, without saying anything else, she walked back to the burlap sack sitting next to the roasting machine. She poured another load of green beans through the top of the barrel-like cylinder and then flipped the power switch back on.

We roasted three full batches before we finally sat at the front counter for our daily dose of *cortadillos*, conversation and coffee. Ramona did not show up that day. In fact, it had been at least four days since I had last seen her. It had been on Monday and we hadn't really talked then either. She had looked a little out of sorts and I had noticed Beatriz had fixed her a *té de tila,* a linden flower tea that my grandmother and mother had always used to calm the nerves. Beatriz and Doña Pilar had not mentioned anything about Ramona to me, but by then I knew them well enough to know that something had happened.

On my way home that afternoon, I intentionally walked past the Tecolote Bar just a few blocks west of the café. The usual drunks were standing outside of the main entrance. Don Julio was a skinny, dark-skinned man with a perpetual, toothless smile on his face and a barely noticeable, patchy beard on his cheeks and chin. His dark denim jeans were always so stiffly starched that I always figured that they stood on their own next to his bed when he took them off at night. Of all the drunks, Don Julio was by far the most tame and harmless.

Then there was Esteban, a fat, lighter-skinned man in his mid-thirties with a skin-tone mole on his right cheek and round eyelash-less eyes. As it oftentimes happened when I was a kid, I always perceived Esteban to be much older than he really was. It was the classic example of age distortion that came along with childhood and adolescent perception. To my fourteen-year-old eyes, people in their thirties, even some in their late twenties, seemed way past the youth mark. Esteban was one of those people. Nobody ever called Esteban by his real name either. He was always referred to as *gordo, botijas, tonelada* or *panzón*. Unlike Don Julio, Esteban had a more perverse look on his face. When I walked past them both on the sidewalk, I nodded briefly in acknowledgement (something I had learned tamed them down even further) and then moved on quickly. Esteban still managed to mumble some incomprehensible comment, but even though I was certain it must have been at least partly lewd, it was incoherent enough where I was easily able to ignore it without too much fuss.

A few steps away from them, I saw two other people crouched on the sidewalk. A cloud of cigarette smoke rose up and away from them as I came closer. Immediately I recognized Ramona from the back. She was sitting next to what seemed like another girl. The girl was talking very animatedly, her hands making dramatic motions in front of her, her voice high and lispy. I was just a few steps away from them when I registered that the girl was in fact a boy, a very effeminate, very dainty and quite pretty-looking boy. I waited a good while for his first break for air before I interjected.

"Hi, Ramona."

She turned around so abruptly upon hearing her name that I could have sworn that I heard her neck pop. By the expression on her face I could tell that I had caught her off guard. It was the first time that we had engaged in any sort of conversation outside of the café and she looked rather uncomfortable.

"Hey." A perfect stream of smoke made its way out of the right side of her halfway open mouth as she handed the cigarette back to Boy-Girl. Boy-Girl took one last drag from the dying, filtered stick and then put it out with the tip end of his flip-flop sandal. Ramona stood up. She placed her hands inside her back pockets and shifted her body weight from her right leg to her left and then back to her right. "What are you doing here, Nena?"

"I just left Doña Pilar's. I'm heading home." I didn't feel the need to explain why I had chosen to take the long way home, past the Tecolote Bar. Ramona probably knew it was because I was worried about her anyway. There was no point in trying to come up with some lame, off-the-cuff excuse. We knew each other too well already.

"Good. This is no place for you." She sat back down on the cigarette-butt littered sidewalk without turning to look at me anymore. I considered walking away for only a brief, almost non-existent second but decided to stretch out my hand to Boy-Girl sitting next to her instead.

"Hi, I'm Ximena." The throaty 'J' sound of the 'X' in my name always sounded much more pronounced when I introduced myself to strangers. He stretched out a delicate hand, palm facing down. For a second I wasn't sure if he was expecting a shake or a kiss on the hand so I opted for a gentle squeeze and shake.

"My birth name is José Carlos, but you won't find anyone here respond to that name." He let go of my hand and pulled out a brand-new pack of Malboro Reds from underneath his left shoulder sleeve. He tapped the sealed box hard against his left palm. "*La Chica de Humo*, that's my name." He opened the pack of cigarettes, pulled one out, placed it strategically between his lips and then flicked open a small, silver lighter. "So, Gee-mena," he intentionally butchered my name as he snapped shut the lighter and stuffed it into his right pocket, "if you address me and expect an answer, you better call for *La Chica de Humo*, the one and only." He snapped his fingers once to the rhythm of "one" and twice to the rhythm of "on-ly." Then he looked away and puckered his mouth until it was no more than a tiny circle from which another steady stream of smoke made its way out smoothly.

"So how have you been, Ramona?" I shifted my attention back to her. *La Chica de Humo* also turned to look at her with a long, annoyed sigh. Ramona smiled at him and the irritation on his face softened a bit.

"My name is actually Sasha now, Nena. Nobody around here knows me as Ramona."

"Oh, I'm sorry." I felt genuinely confused and completely out of the loop. How long had it really been since we had last spoken after all?

"Don't worry about it." She stood up again. "We'll talk later, okay? You should go home. This really is no place for you. You know that."

"Yeah, I know," I said without really knowing.

"Go home," she repeated once again and then directed me down the street like she had always done with the younger girls in our neighborhood. The only difference was that she couldn't fake the stern expression with me. Her face had a gentler look on it as she watched me walk away. At one point, I turned back and saw her wave one last time before she walked back into the Tecolote Bar with *La Chica de Humo*, right past Don Julio and the perverted fatso Esteban.

A strange feeling stuck with me the rest of the way home. I was having trouble digesting the whole name change to begin with, but there was something more, a nagging sense that something else was different, something much more far-reaching than a simple change in moniker. I walked home going over every detail of my brief interaction with Ramona over and over again in my head. As much as I tried, though, I just couldn't pinpoint anything. When I got home close to four o'clock, a meandering headache was already starting to make its way from the base of my neck, up the sides of my head, toward the temples. It was a good thing that Alex had had baseball practice again. For almost a month, he'd had afternoon to late-night practices almost every day so I had spent a lot more time inside my house than usual. I lay down on the couch in the TV room where Elena was watching a pirated version of *Teen Witch*, her new favorite weird-yet-oddly appealing low-budget film. While a visually distorted, staticy-sounding, chocolate-covered Richie Miller taunted Louise with his infamous "Brad, the red-hot lover!" line, I continued trying to make sense of the strange encounter that had just taken place outside of the Tecolote Bar. Before I could conjecture anything, however, I drifted off to sleep. When I woke up an hour or so later to the cringe-worthy rhymes and rhythms of "Top That," my mind felt strangely refreshed. Although Ramona, or rather Sasha, was still in the back of my mind when I walked out to meet with Inez later that evening, it would be almost eight days before she would really take center stage again.

14

Thursday, June 1, 1989

The longer, warmer spring days crept up on us in Nogales in late May, which meant that Inez and I got to see more and more of each other under brightly lit skies even when it was past seven o'clock at night. It had been almost a year and nine months since we had started meeting on a regular basis, sometimes up to three or four times a week. After spending most afternoons with Alex, it was always a nice shift in gears to sit with Inez for an hour or so before heading back inside my house to finish homework and spend time with my own family. The conversations between Inez and me at that point had become completely effortless and, for the most part, she did most of the talking. On my end, I mostly sat and listened and tried to picture in my mind's eye the more liberated and gregarious Inez that she always described in her anecdotes. Mostly they were accounts of her life pre-Prudencio and, regardless of whether they were entirely true or not, I loved listening to them. It was as if somehow they took me to a parallel world, a surreal one that in some ways brought me closer to the core of a culture that resonated deep within me even though I had never fully experienced it myself. Even the intonation of her voice as she weaved together her storylines, the pronunciation of her words in Spanish, failing to enunciate certain *s*-es and using c*h and sh* sounds interchangeably, took me to a different mental space. It was like being immersed into the crux of a rustic yet rich existence that no amount of academic lectures or ethnographic textbooks could ever translate faithfully. On those three or four days out of the week, for just over an hour each day, I would sit next to Inez on the low stone wall that bordered the dense row of shrubs separating our front yards and, under orange, red, bright pink and finally hazy, dark blue skies, I would listen to her describe a life full of sadness and heartache at times, but also brimming with knowledge, verve, passion, and an unwavering strength that, when juxtaposed with the image of Inez that I had upon first meeting her, I would have never imagined possible.

Physically, Inez also looked great during those days. There weren't any bruises or cuts or wounds to begin with. Her brown, smooth complexion glowed in the light of day, bringing out a youthfulness that was clearly still alive and well even in her early forties. Her clothing style also changed during that time. Instead of the rayon flower-print dresses, polyester shirts and elastic-waist pants that she had worn before, she started sporting simple denim jeans and fitted cotton shirts, which surprisingly accentuated a natural, shapely figure underneath. It was during that time that I noticed for the first time just how much Ramona looked like her mother and, in turn, just how beautiful her mother really was.

Inez always seemed very relaxed as she sat and chatted. The tense and awkward silences were long gone and even her mannerisms and gestures flowed with ease. Similarly, I felt very comfortable talking to her about almost anything. Inez was one of the few people with whom I didn't mind talking about Alex. I felt absolutely no reservations telling her how much I enjoyed being around him and how he sometimes made me feel an exhilarating rush that made me tingle all over. For the most part, she would just look at me and smile while I talked about him. Her teeth, the first thing that I noticed in people, were pearly white and so perfectly straight that I couldn't help but ask her once if they were her real teeth. With obvious pride, she smiled wide and nodded yes. After so many blows from Prudencio, I had somehow assumed that Inez would be missing at least a tooth or two. That topic of conversation, however, was still one that we both left untouched. Once or twice I also mentioned how I was friends with Ramona and how I saw her regularly at Doña Pilar's Café, but the manner in which she abruptly changed the subject made it abundantly clear that that was another topic that I was not to raise.

For the most part, though, Inez seemed to relish the moments that we spent together each day. At one point, she started bringing out a blue-and-white-speckled thermos with two matching cups. Sometimes, while we savored her simple yet delicious blend of coffee with evaporated milk and sugar, we would sit in silence and take in the last of the array of colors that the desert sunset painted in the horizon beyond us. Other times she would tell me a little more about her other four children. The oldest were Memo and Pepe. Both had left home in their early teens, long before Inez had even met Prudencio. They did not keep in touch at all and were usually either in jail or on the run. Then there were Ana and Luis, the other two who had refused to move with Inez when she married Prudencio. Even though Inez tried to sound casual and unaffected when she talked about all four of them, there was a sense of emptiness and a hint of grief that clearly manifested themselves in her brown eyes whenever she did. As with Ramona, I learned to pick up a lot more from Inez's facial expressions than I did from her actual words. The vertical creases that formed on her forehead between her brows every time that she talked about her children yelled of the underlying sadness and guilt that were still alive and well in Inez.

When she wasn't in the mood or was not able to continue talking about her family, usually because she was too choked up and did not want to show it, Inez would ask me about mine. Most of the time I felt awkward talking about me and my family because we seemed so boring and dull in comparison. My parents, of course, had had their ups and downs throughout the years and Fernando, Elena and I were certainly not the easiest of kids, but there was really no anger or resentment or pain or any kind of interesting drama to talk about. Somehow that made me feel guilty.

Sometimes when I couldn't fall asleep at night, I would lie in bed and try to think of something tragic or traumatic in my life, something that could make me feel bad or sad, something that could help me relate or feel more connected to Inez and Ramona and all those other people who'd had it so hard. No matter how hard I tried, though, I just couldn't come up with anything. I was a happy kid and, even though I thanked God every night, I couldn't help but feel constantly guilty.

On that Thursday in June, Prudencio's restless snores beckoned Inez back into her house earlier than usual. We had only taken a few sips from our blue-and-white-speckled cups when I noticed an old familiar fear take form on her face. Without saying a word, she threw out the coffee left in her cup, picked up the thermos and ran back inside her house. She closed the door behind her quickly without making any attempts to look back at me. I sat on the stone wall for over ten minutes sipping my coffee ever so slowly in hopes that Inez would make her way back out eventually. Just past the ten-minute mark, I saw Doña Lupita step out of her house across the street instead.

Oftentimes, I had noticed Guadalupe Cordero peeking out of her front living-room window. Sometimes it was when Alex and I were sitting by the water fountain in my front yard. Most often, however, it was when I was sitting on that low stone wall with Inez. She walked out of her house faking a casual step at first. When she realized that I was about to get up and make my way back inside my house, though, she sped up to a quick, almost desperate pace. Before I was fully standing, she plopped herself down next to me.

"So, what is it that you and that woman talk about day after day, huh?" Doña Lupita did not beat around the bush. Her eyes looked fixedly at me. Her face looked far more pale and wrinkled from up close. "She can't be a good influence on good little girls like you," she continued almost choking on her last five words.

It was the first time that words were crossed directly between Doña Lupita and me, no third parties involved to ease the inherent antipathy that existed between us. Although I had never really been interested in her or her life, I did know her story. The truth was that everyone in the neighborhood did. Guadalupe Cordero had never been married but did have three daughters, Clarissa, Corrine and Christina, all from a very well-known local man, who was also very married. In an effort to suppress her demons, Doña Lupita had submerged herself in the Catholic Church and made it her business to scrutinize and harshly judge everyone else's moral missteps in hopes of making her own seem inconsequential. Inez and Ramona had been her easiest targets.

When Inez first moved into the neighborhood, Doña Lupita was quick to befriend her. She rummaged through her pantry looking for old food cans to take over to Inez. Of course, they were never really meant to be heartfelt offerings but only a ticket into Inez's home. During the first couple of weeks, Doña Lupita practically became a fixture inside Inez's house. She scrutinized and questioned everything about Inez, her sudden marriage to Prudencio, her initial refusal to attend church, her unwillingness to talk about her past or her other four children. At one point, after failing to obtain any more personal information directly from Inez, Doña Lupita started inviting Ramona over to her house. Ramona was about a year older than Clarissa, Doña

Lupita's oldest daughter, and although Doña Lupita first invited Ramona under the pretense that she could play with Clarissa, Ramona rarely saw Clarissa or her two sisters during her visits. The few times that she took Doña Lupita up on her invitation, Ramona was only interrogated at length. When she refused to answer Doña Lupita's prying questions, she was asked to leave and was banned from ever going back to look for any of Doña Lupita's daughters. Ramona had no objections. In fact, the only time that Ramona was forced to interact with Clarissa again was when they both had to attend prenatal classes for single teenage mothers at the community center. Ramona was four months pregnant with Nico. Clarissa, who, like her mother, had chosen divine prayer rather than abstinence as her primary, God-approved form of birth control, was seven months pregnant with the first of her six children.

While Doña Lupita looked at me intently from a few inches away that Thursday, I sat quietly looking back at her and contemplating my response to yet another one of her intrusive questions. I could sense her anticipation increase with every passing second. After a minute or two, I finally stood up, pulled out a stick of gum from my right pocket and looked at her coolly. "We talk about the devil," I said matter-of-factly as I popped the stick of spearmint gum into my mouth. "And we also talk about all the evil people who commit adultery and bear false witness against their neighbors." I folded the tinfoil wrapper calmly and slipped it back into my pocket. "Good night, Doña Lupita."

I walked away slowly while her wrinkled face lost the last bit of color left in it. I didn't turn back to look at her a second time but, for my own amusement, I liked to picture her standing up almost unable to hold her balance, her face contorted with a mixture of shock and anger. Just before closing the door behind me, I did hear her condemn me to the deepest layers of hell one more time and I couldn't help but chuckle as I made my way into my house. Not surprisingly, that was also the last time that words were crossed directly between Doña Lupita and me.

Inside my house, my parents were sitting with Isela at the kitchen table. Although I had tried to wipe the mischievous smile off of my face when I walked in, I clearly failed because all three of the adults in the kitchen immediately noticed it.

"What have you done now, *muchachita*?" Isela, like Inez, always randomly swapped the *ch* and *sh* sounds in her words so her pronunciation had really been "moo-sha-shita."

"Nothing," I tried to sound sincere, but the darned smile on my face continued to betray me. Both of my parents were now looking at me inquisitively. "I really didn't do anything," I continued telling them as the annoying, innate good-girl nerves began to kick in. After a few more seconds, they took over me completely. "It was just Doña Lupita," I explained. "She was being nosy and I didn't tell her what she wanted to hear." That was how I chose to phrase it and, essentially, it was the truth. I didn't see any need to go into more detail or itemize exactly what I had said.

My parents seemed content enough with my half-explanation so, after kissing them and Isela goodnight, I headed into my bedroom. I went to bed completely focused on the brief exchange that I'd had with Doña Lupita. I was so consumed by it, in fact, that I never stopped to question what had happened with Inez. Even more distant in my mind was the blue-and-white-speckled coffee cup that I had left sitting on top of the low stone wall that divided Inez's house from mine.

15

Friday, June 2, 1989

It was just past noon, exactly one week since school had let out for summer break, when I walked out of my house en route to Doña Pilar's Café. As usual, I had been the odd one out at home. My mom had been busy translating David Piercy's latest novel in the dining room, which was really more of a makeshift home office than an actual dining room. My dad had left for work at seven o'clock in the morning. Fernando, who had recently gotten his driver's license, had just left for a friend's house and Elena was watching yet another classic '80s flick, that time one with Molly Ringwald in it. Isela napped on the couch next to Elena.

The sun was hanging brightly in the center of the sky above me as I walked across our lawn, past the water fountain and toward the sidewalk. Through the shrubs to my right I noticed someone standing at Inez's front door. At first glance, I thought it might be a Jehovah's Witness dutifully, albeit annoyingly, spreading the Lord's word to the neighbors. As I came closer, though, I immediately recognized Doña Lupita. She stood holding something in her right hand, talking to someone standing just inside the wide-open door. It was at that very moment that the thought of the blue-and-white-speckled cup that had completely escaped me the night before entered my mind for the very first time. It didn't take long for me to figure out that Inez would not be the one standing on the receiving end inside her front door and that the words coming out of Doña Lupita's mouth were certainly not going to be the Lord's. A warm and deadening sensation traveled up the front and back sides of my shoulders as I took a few more steps and then glanced over toward Inez's front porch one last time. Sure enough, Prudencio stood just inside the doorway with his yellowed wife-beater and his greasy face listening attentively to each and every one of Doña Lupita's words.

I continued to walk past them, hoping that I could somehow make it by without being noticed. When I overheard Doña Lupita point me out as "the devil's servant," though, I knew that I had not only been noticed but had also fueled Doña Lupita's rage even further by pretending not to be aware of her and Prudencio. I was walking just past Inez's house into the next-door neighbor's turf when I heard Doña Lupita begin to intonate what, according to her, were a series of exorcism prayers in a foreign tongue, one that sounded nothing like Latin or any other legit language. It was just a bunch of Ts, Rs and Js thrown in together with all sorts of other consonants until it sounded like Doña Lupita was swallowing her own tongue. Even before I fully understood the fundamental rules of linguistics, I knew that the language that Doña Lupita always resorted to when trying to feign a religious trance was completely bogus and made up. Still, I was almost two houses away before her gagging sounds finally died down.

At Doña Pilar's, most of the tables were occupied by a group of women celebrating what appeared to be a bridal shower. Two joined tables on the north side of the café by the big window, where Frank Felix and George Konstantinou always sat, displayed a wide variety of uneaten desserts and dozens of bulkily wrapped gifts. Next to the joined tables, a petite woman with bleached highlights, more than a few thick layers of makeup and a strapless dress stood holding a white umbrella. While the guests took turns standing next to the umbrella-clad dame, a short man in a white shirt and black slacks snapped photograph after photograph of them. I sat at the front counter for a good ten minutes watching the parade of women go by. They all took turns checking themselves out in a compact mirror, applying liberal amounts of lipstick, lip gloss and blush and then making their way next to the bride to strike a superbly unnatural pose. The ones who had clearly gone under the knife already, which was at least one out of every three women, were the most entertaining to see. No matter how hard they tried to pucker or smile or manifest some semblance of a natural emotion, the same freaky, joker-like and synthetic expression was what inevitably appeared before the camera every time the flash went off.

Doña Pilar sat behind the counter by the conical burr grinder and the espresso machine impervious to the synthetic clones that moved about her establishment. She was grinding a small amount of coffee that had just been roasted dark enough to bring out the acidity, but not so dark that the bitterness was overwhelming. The rich smell of the coffee beans inside the café was always at its peak whenever Doña Pilar was grinding. As the extremely fine grounds made their way out of the burr grinder, Doña Pilar took the portafilter from the espresso machine and scooped two full tablespoons of freshly ground coffee into it. She tamped the coffee firmly and then tightened the portafilter back up into the espresso machine. First, she pulled the portafilter handle all the way to the right. After a few short seconds, when the initial noise caused by the building pressure in the machine died down, she slowly moved the handle back to the left until the caramel-colored espresso started to trickle and undulate into her pre-warmed, porcelain demitasse.

Although I had always enjoyed watching Doña Pilar work, that day my attention had been slightly more divided than usual. Most obvious, of course, were the synthetic clones prancing around in real time. Less obvious, but by no means less distracting, was the lingering image of Doña Lupita and Prudencio standing at Inez's front door. That, of all things, was what took precedence in my mind. It bothered me far more than I had initially realized. I sat at Doña Pilar's in silence for several minutes trying to envision the image in my head with more detail. I hadn't actually seen the blue-and-white-speckled cup in Doña Lupita's hand, but by the way she had been clasping on to whatever it was that she was holding, there was little doubt in my mind that it had been the cup. I was also trying to remember if I had actually seen Inez standing further inside the house behind Prudencio. In a burst of wishful thinking, perhaps, I was almost certain that I had seen her silhouette through the doorway when I had taken that last glance. A wave of anxiety started to build throughout my entire body until my limbs felt weak. When I turned my attention back to Doña Pilar, she was already sitting on her stool in front of me, sipping her single shot of espresso as she looked back at me with that ever-present serene look on her face and that subtle knowing smile on her lips.

"There's steam coming out of your ears, child." Her deep, quiet laugh as she spoke was another thing that I had always found very soothing. There was an underlying hum to it, almost like the soft purring of a cat, which seemed almost hypnotic to me. She got up from her stool again, took a bag of linden flower tea from a small, wooden box on the shelf behind her and then poured hot water into a green teacup to let the teabag simmer. "You are too much in your head." She placed the green teacup in front of me. "I always tell Ramona she needs to use her head more, not always let her heart reign. And you, Nena, you must learn to be in your heart more. Learn to trust it like you do your head."

I let the tea sit for a minute and then took a few sips. The naturally sweet herbal flavor of the dried linden flowers stimulated the taste buds as the hot tea made its way slowly down my throat. For a minute, I wanted to tell Doña Pilar everything, what I had told Doña Lupita the night before (which had been all heart, by the way), how I had forgotten the coffee cup on the stone wall and how I thought that Ramona's mother was now in serious trouble all because of me. I wanted to let it all pour out, but before I could say anything, a synthetic clone walked up to the counter next to me to ask Doña Pilar for some forks. By the time Synthetic-Clone made her way back to her party with a handful of stainless-steel forks, my head had taken charge once again and my brief, heart-induced willingness to share had faded.

I stayed at Doña Pilar's for another couple of hours helping her and Beatriz clean up after the bridal shower. While Beatriz cleaned and rearranged tables, I washed dishes and Doña Pilar took care of customers. Although Doña Lupita, Prudencio and especially Inez were still in the back of my mind the whole time, somehow the combination of the linden flower tea and Doña Pilar's contagious serenity had managed to calm my nerves a bit. Before I left, Doña Pilar fixed me a caffé latte with plenty of steamed milk and a frothy milk top inside a wide-mouthed cappuccino cup. She placed it on the counter in front of me and then sat back down on her stool to watch me take the first drink. The velvety smooth milk combined with the rich bittersweet taste of the espresso was surprisingly comforting.

"Pressure is necessary to release the unique flavors and crema of a good espresso, Nena. It strips a coffee to its very core so that you can get to its essence." She pulled out her Partagás Lusitanias cigar and placed it between her lips but did not light it. "Your unique flavors and crema are starting to manifest themselves. Don't be afraid to let them flow." She paused for a few brief seconds, giving me just enough time to interlace the parallel meanings in her words and then continued. "Not everyone will always like them, but those who are truly worth it will develop a taste for them. It would be a real shame if you mute them only to please others, *mon amour*." She closed her eyes, the unlit cigar perched perfectly on the right side of her mouth as she started humming a dulcet tune. Her voice was low, lyrical and nostalgic.

Doña Lupita and Prudencio were nowhere in sight when I walked past Inez's house on my way home. I looked over toward Inez's front porch several times in hopes of at least catching a glimpse of her through the front window. I took small, slow steps as I walked past, but no matter how long or hard I looked there was absolutely nothing to be seen. When I finally reached the edge of my front lawn, a tight knot had already managed to settle in the pit of my stomach and the serenity that I had felt at Doña Pilar's was long gone.

At five till seven, I walked out as usual to meet with Inez. I took my spot on the low stone wall by her mailbox and waited patiently for her to make her way out. Five minutes passed, then ten, then fifteen and all I heard coming from Inez's house was a deep, disturbing silence. I waited another five minutes, the knot in my stomach tightening more and more with every passing second. Finally, I built up the courage to walk over to Inez's front door. I knocked firmly once, then twice. The third time I banged on the door loudly. There was no answer.

I walked over to the front window and thumped on it a few times, as well. Still there was no answer. Cupping the sides of my eyes with my hands, I looked inside through the thinly curtained window. The television set was off and the room looked dark and gloomy. The knot in the pit my stomach was so tight by then that I felt nauseous. After a few more bangs and thumps, I finally decided to go home.

When I turned around, I noticed Doña Lupita's front curtain was slowly closing at one end. A mix of anger but more worry than anything else continued to take a hold of me as I took slow, heavy steps back to my house.

I did not go back out that night, not even after Alex came home from baseball practice. I was much too concerned about Inez. It was only a quarter past eight when I went to bed, the huge knot still stuck in the middle of my gut. I knew that it had been what I had told Doña Lupita the night before that had triggered it all. That was what happened when I let my heart take over, when I let my unique flavors flow. If only I had kept my mouth shut. Tears rolled down the sides of my eyes toward my ears as I lay face-up on my pillow. If anything had happened to Inez, I would never be able to forgive myself. I put my right forearm over my eyes and sobbed softly a while longer until I finally drifted off to sleep.

16

Friday, June 2, 1989, 11:27 p.m.

The doorbell rang several times repeatedly followed by at least ten loud thumps on the front door. I squinted over at the alarm clock on my nightstand. I had been asleep for three hours already. The silence inside the house seemed thicker than usual as the loud thumps filled the air outside. I jumped out of bed and noticed my father was already making his way down the hallway. My heart felt like it was going to jump out of my throat. Behind me, my mom and Isela were also finding their way down the hallway while Fernando peeked out of his room and Elena whimpered half-asleep in our bedroom. My dad had just turned on the front porch light and was looking through the peephole when I recognized Inez's voice outside.

"Nena, it's me!"

My dad opened the front door to find Inez kneeling on the porch before him. She was barefoot and wearing the same T-shirt that I had last seen her with but no pants. Her left eye was bruised and swollen. The biggest shock, however, came when we looked further down to find Ramona lying on the floor in front of Inez, her upper body resting partially on Inez's exposed thighs. Her clothing was also scant and torn, her face a bloody mess.

My father immediately picked up Ramona and carried her inside while my mom and Isela helped Inez in. My father lay

Ramona down on the three-cushion sofa in the living room. Isela held Inez's right side up while my mother supported the rest of her body with an outstretched arm around her waist as they made their way in slowly. I stood in shock just watching them until my mother, somewhat exasperated, had to ask me to call 911. While the dispatcher grilled me with questions over the phone, most of which I really didn't know the answers to, Inez kept mumbling something over and over to herself.

"I did it." Her voice was soft and shaky but still perceptible. "I finally did it." A string of inaudible words continued to pour out of her mouth as her body started to jerk up and down, soft sobs finally finding their way out of her.

The police and two ambulances arrived less than ten minutes later. My mother had already wrapped Ramona and Inez in bathrobes and was tending to their wounds. Apart from the painful gash on her left eye, Inez had red marks across her neck and wrists and her ankles were circled in raw, tender flesh where Prudencio had tied ropes to keep her from leaving the bedroom. Ramona had a busted lip and two deep cuts on the left side of her face just above her eyebrow. Her arms, hands and legs were all scratched up as though she had put up a struggle.

A dozen different officers and paramedics marched in and out of our house for what seemed like an eternity while I stood in a corner watching everything take place as if in a movie, as if in someone else's home, as if in someone else's life. After Inez and Ramona were taken to the hospital, we were all interrogated at length. Even Fernando and Elena who had stayed in their rooms most of the night were questioned.

Outside, red and blue lights lit up the midnight sky as yellow tape was stretched around Inez's house. At least another half-dozen people, some in uniforms, some in suits, marched in and out of her house. A few neighbors stood outside their homes trying to catch a glimpse of what was going on. Ironically, Doña Lupita's pale and wrinkled face was nowhere in sight.

The light of dawn was already visible when the last of the uniforms and suits left our neighborhood. When the big lump covered in a white sheet was wheeled out of Inez's house and into a white van, the huge knot in the pit of my stomach started to turn and a bitter, salty taste filled my mouth. As the white van drove away with Prudencio's lifeless body inside it, I felt the churning move up into my chest and then found myself bent over on the ground finally ridding myself of the wretched knot that had been choking me for far too long.

Inez was released later that same morning, her left eye still swollen and displaying the same blue and dark purple colors that had always settled in a day or two after coming into contact with Prudencio's fists. Despite the physical wounds, however, she looked relieved. For the first time, Inez knew with all certainty that Prudencio would never be laying another hand on her and that her face would most likely never manifest those colors again.

Ramona was kept in the hospital until Sunday afternoon. At first, I didn't understand why she had to stay a day longer or why she needed so many more tests done. When I heard my mom and Inez talking to the doctors, though, a police officer and a man in a suit standing by their side, it became clear that something else was going on with Ramona. While a procession of nosy hospital staff and personnel walked repeatedly past Ramona's room trying to overhear the conversation inside (it was a well-known fact in Nogales that medical privacy was next to non-existent and that the most disturbing rumors and gossip in town were always concocted inside the medical records hallways and offices), I sat by Ramona's bed watching her sleep soundly. Without all the makeup, Ramona still looked like the little girl that in essence she still was. Her skin was smooth and her features very soft. Even with the small gashes above her eyebrow and the puffiness around her eyes and lip, there was something pleasant about Ramona's countenance, an air of innocence and a purity that clashed drastically with the first image that I'd had of her, the same one that still emerged every now and then whenever she was around certain groups of people.

Before we took her home on Sunday, another handful of nurses and health counselors came in to talk to her. They gave her very precise instructions about not lifting any heavy objects or overexerting herself physically, about avoiding alcohol, tobacco and caffeine, about eating foods that were rich in folates, calcium and iron and making sure to take three tablets of folic acid a day. That whole time I sat next to her, listening to the medical staff go over the elaborate instructions and figuring that Ramona had turned out anemic or was coming down with a cold of some sort. It wasn't until the very last counselor gave her an informational pamphlet on prenatal care for teenage mothers that the synapse finally took place in my brain. Ramona was pregnant. She was fifteen years old, two months shy of sixteen, and four weeks pregnant.

It took a while for my brain to fully register the news. Despite all the implications, it was the fact that Ramona was pregnant at all that I found the most shocking. Everyone else, of course, was consumed by the underlying question of who the father was. In the medical records office, it didn't take long for the staff to stir up various, intricately detailed yet completely unfounded stories. The most obvious, of course, was that Prudencio was the father. Then there were also rumors about a few rich and socially well-known men who happened to be regulars at the Tecolote Bar. The man who had fathered Doña Lupita's daughters was included in that latter group, giving Guadalupe Cordero one more reason to resent Ramona.

Inez and Ramona stayed at our house the first week after they left the hospital. The investigation on Prudencio's death was surprisingly quick and short. Based on the injuries on Inez's body it had not been difficult to conclude that she had acted in self-defense. Those of us who knew her a bit more, knew that it had really been her motherly instinct to protect Ramona that had finally pushed her over the edge. Upon seeing Prudencio throw himself at Ramona, she had found the strength somewhere deep inside her to tear the ropes around her hands and feet away from the bed, grab Prudencio's adored pool stick and beat the living pulp out of him.

At home on Sunday, Elena and I each took a couch in the TV room so that Inez and Ramona could sleep in our bedroom. After a weekend of high drama, everyone went to bed extra early. As I lay on the couch listening to John William's *E.T.* score playing softly on the television set, I let out a huge sigh of relief. "Everything's gonna be okay," I whispered to myself. "They're safe now." The words came out of my mouth instinctively, but it took me no more than a few seconds to register that what I was saying was actually true. For the first time, I truly believed that both Inez and Ramona, even Ramona's unborn baby, were all going to be okay.

17

Roasting forges and sculpts the character of a coffee bean. Grinding, which breaks the bean's cellular structure and cuts the bean into very precise pieces, is then required to unlock the flavors sheltered inside.

Sunday, February 23, 2003, 8:23 p.m.

The camera had just moved away from Eminem and onto Aretha Franklin and Bonnie Raitt when I walked back into the TV room. Alex walked a few steps behind me. Mimi looked up lazily at me and then at Alex and then propped her head back onto the cushioned pillow on the two-seater couch completely uninterested. I sat down next to her while Alex took the armchair to my right. I stared at Aretha and Bonnie on the television set and pretended to be engrossed by their words. In fact, nothing was really registering. I was much too focused on Alex. My peripheral vision was on overdrive and I could see that Alex was also unconcerned with the Grammys as he continued looking over at me. I resisted the temptation to look back at him for a record ten seconds before I finally gave in. When I did, his eyes were still fixed on me.

"It's great to see you, Nena." His voice was smooth, his smile disarming. "You don't know how much I've missed this image of you."

I continued looking at him without saying a word. For a brief moment I thought that perhaps the long overdue explanation was finally coming, that the huge void left by the call that never came six years back was finally about to be filled. The anticipation must have been glaring on my face because it took him no more than two seconds to masterfully divert the conversation.

"Do you mind if I have some wine?" He pointed at the bottle of Casa Madero merlot chilling on top of the coffee table.

I got up and walked over to the china cabinet in the dining room where I kept the wine glasses. From the dimly lit dining room, I could see Alex getting up from his armchair, gently picking Mimi up from the couch and then setting her back down on the chair where he had been sitting. When I walked back into the TV room, Mimi was already curled up and lightly snoring in her new spot. She hadn't made the slightest effort to stand her ground. Alex sat on the two-seater couch next to my spot, his smile still thriving.

"I hope it's okay that I took Mimi's spot. It's just that my neck gets really sore when I have to turn to look at the TV for a long period of time." So he still remembered my dog's name and apparently he was also planning on sticking around for a while.

"That's fine," I said as I handed him the wine glass. He stretched out his left arm and my eyes subconsciously veered toward his ring finger. There was no wedding band. I poured his glass full and then took my spot to his left.

We sat quietly watching various artists take the stage, my peripheral vision going full throttle the whole time. Every time Alex brought his glass up to his mouth, which was quite often, I noticed he got a little more comfortable in his spot. He kept spreading out in his space, opening his legs until his left thigh was brushing up against my right. By the time Chris Martin from Coldplay finished his performance, Alex was leaning closely against my right side and a familiar feeling was traveling up and down my spine.

We didn't turn to look at each other for the longest time. We hardly even exchanged words. For the most part, we sat in silence as Norah Jones swept all the big awards. When Alex did budge, it was only to top off his glass again. By the time the big show ended at eleven o'clock, Alex was quite drunk.

The late-night news started at five past eleven and although I initially made an effort to sit through that as well, when I heard the anchor begin to reiterate everything that had already been said during the evening news, I just couldn't bring myself to do it. Besides, after two and a half hours of uninterrupted sitting, my butt was in serious pain. I reached for the remote control and switched off the television set. Just as I was about to get up, I felt Alex's hand grab mine. When I turned to look at him, the expression on his face was unlike any that I had seen before. His eyes were glassy and the grayish-blue color seemed lost under a strange layer of confusion and emptiness. His characteristic smile had also melted off of his face. The self-confident, poised and even a bit arrogant Alex that had been sitting there just a few hours earlier seemed suddenly gone.

"Where are you going?" There was a tone of helplessness in his voice that reminded me quite a bit of the vulnerability and neediness of a teenager, Nico for example.

"I need to pee, Alex." My tone was suddenly more motherly.

"Don't go, please." He pulled my hand toward his chest and then clutched it with both his hands. "Don't leave me."

I looked at him for a few seconds, my head thinking of a million different things that I could respond to his last request. After all, who had left who, really? I sat next to him for another minute or so until I finally managed to liberate my hand from his grasp.

"I'll be right back," I said and walked quickly past him.

When I came back into the TV room, Alex was still sitting on the two-seater couch. At some point during my quick trip to the hallway bathroom, though, he had gotten up and carried Mimi back to the couch with him. He sat slouched on the couch, hugging Mimi, who lay comatose on top of him, and whispering soft somethings into her right ear. Mimi looked momentarily up at me, a bit of confusion perceptible in her eyes. When I sat down next to him on the couch again, he turned around to look at me. His eyes were brimming with tears.

"I've made so many mistakes." His voice was more of a blubber at that point. "How can they ever expect me to fix them?"

"Who?" I asked with genuine curiosity.

"I need to talk to Ramona, Nena." He ignored my initial request for clarification.

"Why?" My curiosity and confusion were increasing exponentially.

"There are things that I need to talk about."

"With Ramona?"

"With a lot of people."

"Like who?"

"Like Lalo and Ramona and you." He was beginning to gain back his composure as I slowly started to lose mine.

"Well, I'm here." I felt somewhat stupid for having to point out the obvious. "What do you need to talk to me about?"

"I have to talk to them first, Nena. Don't ask me why."

I must have looked completely vulnerable and lost as I looked back at him because, despite the terrible shape that he was in, I sensed that he felt even sorrier for me.

Although he was still pretty drunk close to one o'clock in the morning, he refused to sleep on my couch and instead opted for the back seat of his rental car. I walked him to the front door, hoping that he would find it in his heart to disclose a bit more information before leaving, anything that could shed a bit more light on the labyrinth of comments that he had made, anything that could ease the muddle of emotions that he had generated inside me all over again. In fact, not a single word made its way out of his mouth. Not even a goodbye.

I closed the door behind him exactly four hours and forty minutes after he waltzed his way back into my life after six years. I felt completely drained and worn out. When I crawled into bed, however, I couldn't fall asleep. For almost three hours, I rolled around in bed trying to reconcile everything that had taken place that night. My head felt as if it were going to explode. A few times I picked up the phone to call Sasha in Las Vegas but somehow convinced myself each time that it was better to wait. After all, Sasha was coming into town the following weekend. Certainly, I could talk to her about everything then.

The clock on my nightstand had just marked 4:02 in the morning when my head finally gave in and my body finally drifted off to sleep.

18

In the world of research, there are different variables that can influence the outcome of an experiment or study. As indicated by their name, variables are factors that can fluctuate or vary throughout the course of an experiment. In order to gauge the effects of a particular variable upon the end results, a control group is oftentimes used for comparison. In a control group there is little, if any, variation. All factors are typically maintained the same for every trial and, for the most part, they are manipulated by the researcher's hand and will.

In my world, I always considered my life to be a control group, so to speak. Everything was always in check and in balance. There was little room for unexpected change or variation. I never drank too much or ate too much. I exercised regularly. I worked enough but never in excess. I volunteered in various charity and fundraising activities. I spent equal amounts of time with family and friends and strangers and on my own. I read and wrote and reflected on life a lot. I talked and listened just as much. I did everything that I thought necessary and avoided all things that I considered superfluous in order to maintain a rhythm and quality of life that was active and full without being over stimulated or crowded. I thought that I was in control.

Then, like a vague dream that suddenly resurfaces in the middle of the day with succinct detail, I remembered another term from my statistical research class in college: p-value. In layman terms, p-value was the probability that the results for a study were due not to the manipulations or assumptions of the researcher, but merely to chance. It represented the small though viable possibility that, no matter how carefully the researcher thought she had kept all factors and circumstances under control, in the end she really didn't have the last say. Out of nowhere, an unexpected and random variable could still come and pull the rug from under her pretentious and statistically non-significant feet.

A week after they left the hospital, Ramona and Inez moved back into Prudencio's house, sans Prudencio, of course. Ramona healed quite quickly from the physical wounds on her face and body and although it took Inez a bit longer, within a month they were both radiating with health. The glow of pregnancy in Ramona was especially perceptible to the eye. Even without a drop of makeup, her brown skin had a natural glimmer to it and a unique spark was evident in her black, almost violet-looking eyes.

The ironic thing about Ramona's pregnancy was that it was the first and only time in her life that she seemed to fully enjoy being a kid, albeit a pregnant one. It was the only time that she let herself be taken care of without feeling guilty or irresponsible. Every day Inez would prepare either *cocido*, *cazuela*, *sopa juliana*, *consomé de pollo*, *gallina pinta* or another one of her hearty soups for her and then at night she would rub her belly, hips and lower back with a blend of mashed carrots, grape pulp and field horsetail. During her first two trimesters, Ramona also attended high school equivalency classes at the community center where she was taking her prenatal classes. By the time she rounded her fifth month, when the bump in her belly finally started to make itself present, she had already earned her general education development certificate.

Although Ramona's passion had always been the art of creating unmatched drinks behind the bar, when she found out that she was pregnant, Ramona knew that she could not go back to the smoke-plagued Tecolote Bar. Besides, even before the incident with Prudencio, there had been a sudden change in the air at the Tecolote Bar. Something had happened that had made Ramona recoil from the environment there. Usually, she had loved to talk about her work. During the last weeks, though, since I had seen her looking a bit out of sorts at Doña Pilar's, she had refused to talk about anything having to do with it. My first assumption, of course, was that it had something to do with the rumors that had started circulating about the father of her baby. She knew that a few of the patrons were being singled out and, in an attempt to avoid the topic altogether, she steered clear of anything having to do with the bar.

At first, when the rumors were at their thickest, I couldn't help but wonder why Ramona chose to keep quiet about who the real father was. To me it seemed so much easier to clear the air than it did to have to withstand all sorts of glares and rude or tongue-in-cheek comments from strangers. Even Doña Lupita, whose daughter was a year younger than Ramona yet was further along in her own pregnancy, didn't miss a chance to call Ramona all sorts of irreligious names. At the end of the first few months, though, when I started to witness the miraculous things happening to Ramona's body, my focus went to an entirely different place. As I saw her belly expand, her breasts ripen and later felt the percussion of the little life forming inside her, I couldn't care less who the sperm contributor had been. It seemed entirely irrelevant. What mattered was that Ramona looked her happiest. Despite all the mean-spirited blather that continued to swarm around her, Ramona flourished throughout her entire pregnancy. Even on the day that Nico was born, as she endured fourteen long hours of labor, she looked big, round, beautiful and full of life.

Nico was born in February, just six days before my own birthday. He was born with a full head of hair that, like Ramona's, was so dark that under certain light it gave off gleams of blue. His skin, on the other hand, was much fairer. It was a very light-caramel color that throughout most of his childhood years earned him the nickname *Café con Leche*. His eyes at first were also almost as dark as his hair. As he grew older, though, they slowly started to lighten in color until they looked almost a yellowish-brown whenever he wore light-colored clothing.

During the first couple of weeks after Nico was born, I found it hard to be away from him for long periods of time. He was born shortly after Alex had left for college and in a way Nico seemed to fill the void that Alex's departure had left. When I came home from school, after a quick visit to Doña Pilar's and an even quicker trip to my house, I would go straight to Inez's house. Right at around 4:30, while Inez and Ramona enjoyed a late-afternoon nap, I would take Nico from his bassinet, wrap him snuggly in a soft cotton receiving blanket and then rock him back and forth in Inez's old rocking chair for almost an hour. While he slept, I loved examining every little part and every last detail about him: his perfectly delineated lips; his stubby little nose; his flawlessly shaped fingernails; his random, fleeting smiles; his soothing, clean baby smell. I could sit there for an entire hour completely intrigued and fascinated by the miracle that Nico embodied for me.

The bond that developed between Ramona and Nico during those first years and especially the first few months was also something magical to see. Every time that Ramona held Nico in her arms, I could see that rare part of her that was never seen around other people. It was an openly tender and completely unguarded side of her. A few times I noticed her eyes fill up with tears as she looked at him almost unable to believe how lucky she was to have him. Nico's soft cooing sounds and his placid little smile as he looked back at his mother were sometimes enough to make my own eyes water and my heart overflow with tenderness. That touching image of Ramona and Nico, a sixteen-year-old child enveloping her own defenseless child in her arms, was one that stuck with me for the longest time.

Four months after Nico's birth, Ramona went back to work in order to supplement the small and continuously waning amount of money that Prudencio had left. Although the job at the Tecolote Bar was always waiting for her, upon Inez's request, Ramona took a job at a *maquiladora* in Nogales, Sonora instead. From six o'clock in the morning to six o'clock at night from Monday to Saturday, Ramona stood next to almost 320 other men and women in white lab coats and goggles and pieced together small nuts and bolts onto halfway-assembled carburetors. At the end of an almost seventy-hour workweek, with her feet aching from standing all day and her fingers cut and chafed from manipulating the small metal parts, she would take two *peseros* back to the border and bring home her two-hundred-and-fifty-dollar check. When she got home at close to eight o'clock at night, she would be too tired to do anything other than lay down for a few minutes next to Nico, who was usually already asleep. She would then have a small bite to eat and then head back to her bedroom for a few hours of sleep before getting up again at 4:30 in the morning and beginning another identical day. For two and a half years the same routine shaped Ramona's days.

At the end of the first year, I could easily see the toll of the humdrum rhythm of her life in Ramona's face. The natural glow of her skin and the sparkle in her eye seemed to slowly vanish behind thick layers of disillusion and an almost palpable despair. When I visited with her on Sundays, the only day out of the week that she didn't work, I struggled to find remnants of the charismatic and vibrant Ramona that I knew. She looked much thinner than I had ever seen her and the expression on her face was always weary. Whenever she held Nico, the struggle within her became most obvious to me. I could tell that she wanted to be a good mother, one that Nico could be proud of, and she also wanted to please Inez, but no matter how diligently she followed Inez's recommendations, Ramona felt more and more like a failure each day. One painful stab after the other, she was slowly butchering her spirit to death and that was hardly something that she felt Nico would be proud of.

Still, Ramona endured the grueling and badly remunerated work at the factory for over two years. A few months before her twentieth birthday, I sat with her on the wooden rocking chairs that Inez had placed outside of their house in place of the rusty folding chair that Prudencio had always sat on. Nico sat comfortably on Ramona's lap, his head gently leaning against her chest as she rocked him back and forth slowly. It was a Sunday and while Inez had gone to church earlier in the morning, we had gone to Doña Pilar's. We had sat at the front counter as always, Nico sleeping in his stroller next to Ramona. It was the first time that Ramona had gone to the café in a long time and as she watched Beatriz and Doña Pilar work, I had noticed the expression on her face change. As Doña Pilar ground and blended and steamed and poured, I saw Ramona's attention peak. Her eyes had been wide as they followed every one of Doña Pilar's motions.

When we made it back to her house close to one o'clock, the same animated expression was still painted all over her face. As we sat side by side on her front porch, I could sense the renewed energy buzzing inside her. She never said a word, but when she turned to look at me, the long-lost spark suddenly re-emergent in her black eyes, I knew that her decision had been made. I looked back at her with a subtle air of complicity. Then, without realizing when Doña Pilar ended and I began, the long-simmering allegories started to flow.

"We're just like coffee beans, Ramona. We can't be pushed into becoming what's not in our nature. If you've found the roast that brings out the best in you, the perfect path for you to express yourself, then don't be afraid to follow it."

19

Ramona quit her job at the factory the following Monday. On Tuesday she started working the day shift at the Tecolote Bar. At first, she told Inez that her schedule had been changed at the factory, no more early mornings or late nights. When she started bringing home more money, she lied once again and told Inez that she had been promoted to a floor manager position. Although she never felt entirely comfortable lying to Inez, Ramona knew that Inez would never approve of her decision to go back to the bar. Despite the changes and growth that had taken place in Inez, there was still a part of her that held on tightly to certain customs and traditions and, no matter how hard she had tried to break away from the resulting social pressures, in many ways they still dictated how she lived her life and, in turn, how she wanted Ramona to live hers.

For almost a year, Ramona maintained the same facade before Inez, each day feeling the weight of her lies heavier and heavier on her shoulders. Sometimes when she saw in Inez's face a certain expression of pride and even trust, Ramona felt a piercing pain turn in her stomach and an asphyxiating guilt took over her soul. A few times Ramona came close to telling Inez the truth, but the fear of being judged and turned away like she had been years back when she had told Inez about Prudencio's

1416171819202122232425262728293031323334353637383940

inappropriate gestures and touching was much too great to allow her to come clean.

At the Tecolote Bar, however, Ramona was in her zone. From ten o'clock in the morning to six o'clock at night when she finished her shift, Ramona was able to forget about her troubles and the stress of her life outside of the bar. As she mixed and stirred new and old drink creations for the clientele, Ramona's spirit entered a different realm. Her hands seemed to have a mind of their own as they moved about, bringing to life the different recipe ideas that overflowed in her head, each one with a new twist. A sprinkle of sugar here, a dash of pepper there, a few drops of honey, a splash of lime juice, a couple of fresh peppermint leaves, a pinch of nutmeg, the possibilities were boundless.

After preparing the drinks, what Ramona enjoyed the most, by far, was watching the customers take that first drink. The expression that formed on their faces as they brought the glass to their mouth for the first time was the most pure and unbiased indication for Ramona of the quality of her work. That was how she measured her success. Unfailingly, the expressions were as close to ecstasy as Ramona had ever seen and, no matter how hard she tried to replicate that same response in people in other areas of her life, she never felt as capable or accomplished as she did behind the bar.

After her first month back, the number of patrons who visited the Tecolote Bar regularly increased twofold. Ramona's charm and charisma were thriving once again. Even though she wasn't quite twenty yet, still a year and a few months too young for the job, the same makeup and fake ID tricks that had worked when she was only fourteen and a half were enough to get her back on board. What was more, even though many of the customers knew of her due to the scandalous incident with Prudencio a few years back, most did not care one bit about her real age. What mattered to them was her unmatched ability to stir up one magnificent drink after the other. For those customers who should have cared, a handful of local government officials included, a fat wad of cash from the owner was enough to convince them to look the other way.

For just over a year, Ramona enjoyed working at the Tecolote Bar during the day and spending vast amounts of time with Nico during the mornings, evenings and weekends. Thanks to her wages at the bar, and especially to the generous tips from her customers, Ramona was also able to provide for Nico and Inez with much more financial freedom during those days. Just before Nico's fourth birthday, Ramona bought her very first car. It was the 1988 four-door silver Nova. For Nico's birthday, she drove us up to see the Grand Canyon. Inez, who felt queasy at the simple thought of seeing the canyon depths, opted to stay behind in Nogales. I, on the other hand, left school early on Friday to take the four-hundred-mile drive up to Grand Canyon Village with Ramona and Nico.

The backdrop of the Arizona winter as we drove up that chilly Friday in February was almost as breathtaking as the Grand Canyon itself. Except for the seventy miles of flat and almost barren land between Picacho Peak and Phoenix, the landscape that circled around us was a perfect illustration of the charm and enchantment of the Southwest. There were the green-covered Arizona ash and black walnut trees swaying softly in the crisp coldness near Tubac, the snow-topped saguaros lining the roads along Flagstaff, the bright oranges and yellows penetrating through the deep, icy blue splendors in the sky, the humbling heights of millennium-old mountains casting dancing shadows in the distance. Throughout the entire drive up, as the sun changed positions and transformed shadows and colors in the sky, the same fascinating drama of nature staged itself all around us.

From Flagstaff, we took Interstate 40 west to Highway 64, just east of Williams. On Highway 64 we headed directly north toward the south entrance of the Grand Canyon's South Rim. When we entered the National Park just a few minutes before five o'clock, the warm golds and reds of sunset were already starting to take their positions in the horizon. Ramona drove past Grand Canyon Village toward Hermit Road. When we finally reached Mohave Point, the normally quiet view of the inner canyon was ablaze with color. The buttes and pinnacles illuminated from below portrayed a spectacular show of lights, silhouettes and texture. As I stood mesmerized by the gripping universe around me, a warm feeling of gratitude came upon me. When I turned to look at Ramona, her arms firmly holding onto Nico as they contemplated the spectacle before them, the feeling multiplied inside me. Ramona looked complete. For the briefest of moments, just before the darkness of night stole the last of the oranges, reds and pinks from the sky, Ramona was whole.

We arrived back in Nogales on Sunday close to seven o'clock at night. Sunrise at the Grand Canyon had been calm and clear yet, by mid-morning, a persistent breeze had started to stir dust into the atmosphere. By the time we drove through Flagstaff at around one o'clock in the afternoon, a strong wind had kicked in and a dense patch of cloud cover had taken over the sky above us. When we drove into Nogales, a cold and dreary drizzle was falling.

When Ramona pulled into her driveway, I immediately noticed the front door to the house open. Inez stepped out onto the porch. She was wrapped in a thick, light-pink robe. I got out of the car and carried Nico inside. He had fallen asleep shortly before we had entered Tucson. Ramona grabbed the two small duffel bags from the trunk and followed behind me. I greeted Inez briefly as I walked past her but didn't wait for her response. Nico was heavier than I remembered and getting him to his bed was my priority. Besides, the bulky collar on Inez's robe had covered most of her face. Even if I would have wanted to see her expression, it would have been hard to find behind the thick layer of light-pink synthetic wool.

I tucked Nico in and then walked back into the front room where Inez and Ramona were still standing. Ramona still held onto my duffel bag in one hand as she clutched onto hers in the other. They barely noticed me walk back into the room. Ramona's expression was suddenly aghast. She looked completely dumbfounded and, as the dark caramel color of her complexion started to drain right out of her body, an unexpected vulnerability took over. Her semblance was exactly the opposite from the one that I had seen just two days before at Mohave Point. She looked irremediably broken and the wholeness that had been almost tangible on her face before was replaced with an agonizing emptiness.

The expression on Inez's face was just as hard to take. Although I'd seen her face physically hurt and wounded many times before, the emotional pain visible on her face that night was unlike anything that I had seen before. The deception and anger were the most obvious, of course. More obscure were deep-rooted feelings of helplessness, love and concern which clashed violently with her anger and tore her soul into jagged, painful pieces. Over the last few years, Ramona and Nico had become the center of Inez's life and she could not bear the thought of either one of them being hurt again.

It didn't take long to conclude that Doña Lupita had been around to stir dust into the otherwise calm and clear atmosphere over the weekend. Although Doña Lupita had kept her distance shortly after Prudencio's death, after the first year, when she found out that her still single eldest daughter was pregnant again, she went back to her venomous ways. In an attempt to veer the attention off of her family once again, she started scrutinizing every one of Ramona's actions. For two years she kept a sharp eye on Ramona, following her to the bus stop in the mornings and then waiting for her to come home from the factory late at night. For two years she desperately looked for something sinister in Ramona's life, anything that could help tarnish Ramona's already fragile reputation in the neighborhood. When she wasn't able to find anything, she grew increasingly frustrated until she finally gave up for a while.

When Ramona started working at the Tecolote Bar, Doña Lupita was too busy dissecting the lives of all the other women and girls in the neighborhood to notice. It wasn't until a week before our trip to the Grand Canyon, while Doña Lupita was spying on the seriously inebriated father of her daughters outside of the Tecolote Bar, that she noticed Ramona leaving her shift at the bar. For four days, she followed Ramona to and from work. Then, early on Sunday morning, aware of the fact that Ramona's car had not been parked in the driveway all weekend long, she slithered her way across the street and let her lethal poison seep right into Inez.

Inez was furious at Ramona for a long time. Before I left their house that Sunday night, she asked Ramona to leave. From that back part of the front room where I had been standing, I watched as Ramona dropped my duffel bag to the floor, turned around and, without saying a single word, walked back out of Inez's house. It was the last time that she made her way through that doorway for well over a decade.

20

Monday, March 24, 2003

A month after Alex unexpectedly dropped by my house in Tucson, the announcement arrived. He was being named secretary of state, second in line of succession to the governor. Through various media outlets once again, I was forced to read, see and hear about Alex Piercy over and over again. Ironically, the most interesting piece of news for me came from the Nogales newspaper, a non-daily paper with circulation of less than thirty-five hundred.

On the front page as usual, there was a huge photograph of Alex smiling in a dark suit and a Southwestern-patterned tie. Although the entire front page was dedicated to him, the story that caught my attention was on page four. It was actually a letter to the editor. The author had signed *"Slugger29"* and, in the content of his letter, he questioned the true nature and character of the newly appointed secretary of state. *Slugger29*, an old baseball teammate of Alex's, was quick to recognize the native politician's natural allure and charisma. More evident, however, was his aversion to Alex's "duplicitous ways" and his "disregard for human sensibility." Although he did not go into much detail, the understated manner of the letter, despite the brazen choice of language, gave the writing an underlying sense of credibility. I read the letter several times, each time finding each short paragraph more sizeable in meaning than the last.

Over the course of the next few days, the letter gave way to a tornado of comments. The vast majority, of course, were in favor of the local luminary. One after the other, the comments passionately, even if only anecdotally, defended Alex's name and honor while tagging *Slugger29* as a spiteful and jealous fellow. In the meantime, while all sorts of Nogalians took turns stepping up in Alex's defense, a bigger set of news slowly started boiling over elsewhere.

On Friday morning, the news appeared on every newspaper, television channel, radio station and Internet website in the United States. Alex Piercy, the young and charismatic Arizona secretary of state who was married to Senator Joseph Matthews' daughter, was being accused of having an extramarital affair. The woman in question, the one captured in all the incriminating middle-of-the-night, grainy photographs: Sasha Valencia, a well-known Las Vegas topless dancer.

The photographs appeared everywhere. There were three different pictures and, based on the clothes that they were wearing, all three photos seemed to have been taken on the same night. Alex wore a dark blue pair of loose-fit denim jeans and a black turtleneck sweater. Sasha wore matching dark gray leggings and a wool sweater with a black scarf and a pair of black boots. In the first two pictures, Sasha faced away from the camera so for a minute I doubted that it was really her. In the third photograph, however, although her face looked downward, I immediately recognized the gray knit beanie that she had worn on her last trip to Tucson. It was definitely Sasha walking into The Venetian Hotel in Las Vegas with Alex.

As with most political scandals, after the initial shocking claim, new details were slow to surface. Instead, the same tired photographs and redundant information were recycled on every news network and media outlet for hours. Even the Nogales newspaper printed a short piece on the subject in the bottom left-hand corner of the third page in the Friday paper. Suddenly, *Slugger29*'s claims did not seem quite as outlandish as they had a few publications back, but true to a culture that encouraged its people to overlook the gargantuan elephant in the room, no one ever bothered to write another commentary or touch on the subject again.

On Friday evening, Alex's spokeswoman made the traditional vague statement that was typical of all meandering politician scandals. Perhaps not in so many words nor using the same qualifiers that I would have chosen, the spokeswoman asked the public to be considerate of the secretary of state's difficult position (one he had single-handedly put himself in), respectful of his family (even when he himself had not) and nonjudgmental of his actions (no matter how scummy they had been). I listened to the masculine-looking woman with a blond bob and glasses speak behind the podium and was surprised to see how unaffected I was by the words coming out of her mouth. As a matter of fact, nothing about Alex seemed to penetrate past my skin. Not his name, his position, his overrated charisma, his glorified smile nor anything else having to do with him were enough to trigger a single reaction in me. It was like firing lethal shots into already dead matter.

When I listened to Sasha's voice on my answering machine later that night, however, an all-too-familiar pang of heartache ripped through my soul once again. With unexpected force it yanked me back from the safety of my temporary emotional death and hit me harder than anything that I had ever felt before. The heartache that I had experienced with Alex six years back paled in comparison to the new feeling of betrayal. As I listened to Sasha's small, almost inaudible voice asking for forgiveness on my answering machine, a crippling pain penetrated deep inside me. It was like a razor-sharp dagger skillfully slicing through my most profound sensibilities, leaving my heart butchered and raw. I listened to the message more than fifteen times, studying her tone and inflections with painful detail. No matter how carefully I listened, though, I just couldn't read through her voice. Was her apology an indirect admission of her betrayal? Was she really having an affair with Alex? I picked up the phone to call her just as many times, but no matter how badly I wanted to hear her tell me that none of it was true, that it was all a lie propagated by a sensationalist media, I couldn't bring myself to talk to her.

During the next few days, I couldn't turn the television set on either. The images of Alex and Sasha being played and replayed over and over again on almost every channel, from E! to CNN, filled me with a nauseating feeling that made it difficult for me to breathe. Then there were other images and video clips of Sasha that also started making the rounds. Some were old photographs of her dressed in her full (although scant) yellow-feathered dance attire. Two blurred circles covered her otherwise exposed breasts. The video snippets, which had been taken on Friday night after the news had broken, showed Sasha walking through some sort of parking lot as a horde of photogs pushed and hovered around her, the expression on her face visibly frightened and confused. That was the hardest part of it for me.

Although the news would have stung regardless of who the female lead would have been, what made my pain almost unbearable was the fact that I could not resort to hatred or cruel schemes of revenge as outlets for my suffering. No matter how much I was hurting, there was an underlying sense of respect and affection for the protagonist that I did not dare break. It was that clash of emotions, that tug of war between my genuine concern and empathy for Sasha and a deep feeling of resentment that jerked at my heart strings and tore my soul brutally in two. Sasha had always been the one I turned to whenever I hit some kind of bump in the road. She had been the one to see me through every crisis. Whether it had been Yahdyrah or Alex or anyone else who rudely or callously crossed my path, it had always been Sasha to step in and help soothe my bruised and tender feelings. Suddenly that lifeline was gone.

On Saturday morning, my mom and dad drove up from Nogales. There was no describing how the simple sight of my mother (her 5'4" delicate frame; her smooth, washed face; her big, brown eyes; her soft, dark hair falling just above her shoulders) could fill me with such a deep sense of serenity. She was a beautiful woman with a simplicity and warmth that radiated from every pore in her body. Even before she uttered a single word, the simple feel of her hand on my cheek and her soft scent of ylang ylang and bergamot made my spirit feel ten times lighter. For the briefest of moments, my parents' presence was enough to help me forget just how much I was hurting. As I leaned into my mother's arms, I felt something inside me release and before I knew it, I was crying my twenty-eight-year-old wounded heart out like a child of two, my father gently patting my back. After that initial deluge, the tears just kept on coming.

On Sunday night, my mother packed a small duffel bag with a few toiletries and some changes of clothes for me. Wearing the same pajamas that I had been wearing since Friday night (and the same ones that would remain on my body for the next five days), I took Mimi under my right arm and climbed into my father's blue Jeep Cherokee. Both Mimi and I slept the entire way back to Nogales. On Monday morning, for the first time ever, I called in sick to work. It was the first time that I wasn't able to pull myself out of bed, something that I had done even when I had been running a 101-degree temperature or had a pounding migraine or had food poisoning that kept me running to the bathroom all day. The physical maladies, I had always been good at keeping under control, no matter how inconvenient or uncomfortable. The new emotional afflictions that I was feeling, however, were a completely different story.

For five days straight, I did not leave the bedroom that Elena and I had shared as kids except for a few counted trips to the bathroom. As I lay in bed either sleeping away the profound sadness that clung stubbornly to my heart or chasing away the pain of a disenchanted reality with a never-ending stream of tears, I saw the light of day appear before my window and then disappear indifferently again. The natural cycles of life continued forth unaffectedly even as I lay powerless to my own thwarted life. The hours also seemed to play warped games with my perception. They seemed strangely short at times, yet in the bigger timeline of my life they did not seem to make even the smallest of dents. The same heaviness that I had felt upon hearing Sasha's voice on my answering machine several days back was still as real and as crushing as if I had only heard it a few minutes back.

In that altered state of consciousness, torn between a distorted dream world and a hazy reality that oftentimes seemed more like a vague dream, I could hear the telephone and the doorbell ring in the background. Sometimes I could hear the muffled sound of voices coming from the living room. Even though I could recognize most of the voices (Inez, Marcela and David, Doña Lupita and one of her daughters, even Yahdyrah), I never felt motivated to see or talk to any one of them. Subconsciously, I was listening for Sasha's voice. My ears were primed to hear her tenor and pitch. She was the one that I would have let in. Even though I had avoided her early on, as I lay helpless in bed, she was the one person that I wanted and needed to see.

The days passed, however, and Sasha's voice never made its way to my ears. Elena flew in from Los Angeles where she had been living and working for three years already. Fernando flew in from San Juan in Puerto Rico where he had opened his own architectural firm. Even my cousin Piru managed to fly in from Guadalajara where he had studied and gotten married. Sasha, however, never made her way down to Nogales.

On Friday morning, exactly one week after the news had first broken, I woke up facing the window on the east side of the bedroom. The wooden shutters blocked out most of the sunlight. On a small table next to the nightstand, I could see that Isela had brought in yet another corn quesadilla for me. She had made me take at least a bite or two from each one that she had brought in throughout the week. That time, however, next to the cold quesadilla was a varied selection of Mexican pastries, and next to the pastries was a coconut shell with a small note attached to it. Instinctively, I reached for the coconut shell first. It was empty. I unpinned the note and opened it. Doña Pilar's childlike handwriting moved across the small piece of paper sloppily.

It is time to fill it up with a new blend. Time to break away from your old shell. To discover superior and more intense flavors. –P

I set the shell back on the table and, before I could throw myself back onto the bundled pillow, I heard someone speak behind me.

"Good morning." Lalo sat in a wooden chair a few feet away from the bed, his right hand cradling a blue pen. A tattered, leather journal lay open on his left crossed thigh.

"What are you doing here?" I couldn't help sounding startled.

"Doña Pilar asked me to bring you some coffee." He stood up and walked back out of the room. I saw as he made his way down the hallway toward the TV room that led into the kitchen. Less than two minutes later he made his way back through the hallway and into the bedroom, a steaming terra cotta mug in his hand. He handed it to me and then sat back down on the chair next to my bed.

"How long have you been here?" The soothing, earthy scent of the coffee rising from the terra cotta mug was not enough to chase away the awkwardness of finding Lalo guarding over me as I slept.

"A little while," he said noticing the discomfiture in my face. "Don't worry, you didn't do anything embarrassing." His lips widened into a warm, almost shy smile and for the first time in over a week I felt a smile form on my own face. "Drink your coffee," he looked away from me and back down onto his leather journal, the shyness gleaming more than before.

I sipped on the heavenly blend in the mug and immediately noticed a distinctively superior flavor in the coffee.

It had a sweet, caramelized-sugar taste and the body was substantially fuller than what I had always drank before. It was a Vienna roast.

"Doña Pilar roasted some of her *Perla de Xoconostle* beans just for you. She said they remind her of you. That you can both withstand higher-degree roasts."

I took another joyous swig from the coffee mug and then looked over at Lalo again. That time he continued looking at me. He didn't turn away. Strangely, I didn't either. For the first time ever, I was able to look into Lalo's eyes without feeling the pressure of having to look away or change the subject to avoid feeling exposed or vulnerable. After the week that I'd had, it was practically impossible to feel anything other than exposed and vulnerable and, suddenly, it didn't seem quite as terrible.

"What are you writing?" I gestured over at his journal.

"I'm revising some of the chapters in my novel for my editor. He says I tried so hard not to be over-romantic or sappy that the story's now as dry and stiff as cardboard." He laughed softly again and I noticed the outline of his lips for the first time. Usually, I was too concerned or distracted by the apparent sarcasm that curled the corners of his fleshy lips. As I looked closer at him then, however, I noticed how pleasant his smile really was.

"What's your novel about?"

"Coffee," he said as he leafed through some of the pages in his journal. Then he looked back up at me. "And love."

He looked at me a while longer and I suddenly felt a hint of the good, old-fashioned nerves stir up in my stomach. Before I let them take too strong a hold of me, I took another sip of coffee and continued the conversation. "You sound like Doña Pilar."

"Yeah, well she's definitely one of my muses." He continued looking at me, his olive-green eyes gentle and warm on my face. I took another long sip. Then another. And yet one more. Finally, his voice broke through the silence again. It was just as gentle and warm. "Listen, Nena, I'm really sorry for everything that you've been through."

Straightaway, I felt a tight knot take residence in my throat again. It was like being heaved back into the depths of a sordid and torturous reality that I had somehow managed to escape from for the briefest of moments. I looked at Lalo and felt the tears filling my eyes and blurring my vision of him. I tried keeping it together a while longer, but the steadfast tears kept building in my eyes and the temporarily subjugated sobs began violently piercing my throat. When they both finally found their way out of me, Lalo got up from the wooden chair he had been sitting on and found a spot next to me on the bed. He wrapped both arms around me and the next thing I knew I was crying my heart out all over again. That time nestled in the soothing, subtle, aftershave-scented groove on the left side of Lalo's neck.

21

After the first week at my parents' house, I called in sick to work a second week. The head of the department, who was my direct supervisor, pretended to be considerate of my situation but then requested that I be back at work on Friday. Some Spanish-speaking scholars were set to visit our campus that day and she would need a translator, a monetarily uncompensated task that had become my unspoken responsibility in the department. While my mother made almost half of my annual salary in a week with her translations, I got a few pats on the back and maybe an overly buttered-up acknowledgement or two in the weekly faculty meeting. The funny thing was that for the longest time that really was enough for me. Even though I knew that it was really just a very polite and diplomatic way of exploitation, I never really took offense to it back then. Just like I never took offense when the same department head asked me and another colleague, who happened to be Native American, to be extra careful while driving the university vehicle. A police officer, she explained, might find it suspicious to see two Mexican women in a car with state government license plates. The kicker was that she genuinely thought that she was being not only politically correct and broadminded but helpful. As I sat in my bed in Nogales that second week, my injustice radars more sensitive than usual, I couldn't help feeling retroactively annoyed. Still, I agreed to be back at work on Friday.

After my last meltdown with Lalo, I finally managed to make it into the shower and, after that day, I made it out of the bedroom for at least a few hours each day. Mostly, I sat in the Arizona room that looked out toward our backyard and the Coronado National Forest in the horizon. In the distance, I could also see toy-sized semi-trucks passing back and forth along Mariposa Highway, their cargo boxes colorfully advertising the watermelons, cantaloupes, tomatoes or other produce that they transported all day long to and from the border.

Being back in Nogales after being away for almost ten years was a rather mind-boggling experience. Although I had visited many times before, they had always been short visits, maybe one or two days tops. Somehow in my mind, I had already categorized myself as a Tucsonan and, although Tucson was not considered a traditional big city, it was big enough where being back in Nogales felt something like jumping back from a pond into a fish bowl.

It was strange to see how much things didn't change, how customs and routines remained practically intact and unaltered over time. At 6:30 in the morning the next-door neighbor's gardener was already pruning rosebushes and bougainvilleas while the radio in his truck played loud *norteño* music that was thick with circus-like accordions and high-pitched, nasally voices. Inside our house, I could smell the mix of sautéed onions, tomatoes and serrano peppers that Isela added to practically every breakfast dish that she prepared, from *chilaquiles* to *huevos rancheros* to *fritanga*. At around 6:45, the soft scent of *Carolina Herrera for Men* would slowly start to make its way from my parents' bedroom down the hallway toward the other bedrooms. When my father finally left for work, the clean smell of his cologne would linger throughout most of the back part of the house. Even the crackling sounds of the ceiling and wallboards adjusting onto the thirty-year-old wooden house frame seemed timelessly familiar.

Although most of those peculiarities would have normally gone unnoticed before (so obvious that they were the easiest to overlook), as I struggled to regroup my disrupted world back into one whole piece, I found them oddly reassuring. It was as if they were small pieces forming part of the larger puzzle of who I was and where I came from, as if carefully matching them up could help me find myself and my identity again.

After that one Friday, Lalo started bringing me coffee from Doña Pilar's every morning. He would then sit in the wooden rocking chair next to me in the Arizona room and work on his novel in silence while I drank my Vienna roast and savored the tranquility of the mountains and the birds and the bright-blue skies that hung in the space before us. Sometimes he would read short pieces of his writing to me and ask for my opinion. Halfway through my words, he would start scribbling away again as if trying to capture whatever thoughts had just entered his mind on paper before they vanished. At around noon, he would leave to teach his literature class at the local alternative high school, but early the next morning, by eight o'clock, he would be back with an insulated coffee thermos in one hand and his tattered leather journal in the other.

On Friday morning, Lalo was the one to drive me up to Tucson in his good ol' Chevy S10. He was leading a writing workshop at the Downtown Campus of Pima Community College at eight o'clock so he dropped me off in front of the psychology building at the university at 7:40. I was twenty minutes early. When I walked into the department office, I immediately noticed the off-putting smell of stale coffee. I walked over to the coffee percolator in the waiting hall and opened it to find several-days-old coffee swishing around inside with a crusty, burnt residue stuck all around the stainless-steel case. For a minute, I considered taking the percolator back and washing it like I had always done before. As I stood there realizing how much I did not want to be there and how much I really hated cleaning up after everyone else, I made a final decision. I walked into my five-by-eight office, piled up all of my case files and personal belongings into a box and walked out of the psychology building for the last time.

Over the course of the next few months, I made contact with the last few people (previously denominated "subjects") in my caseload and submitted all final budgets and reports to my grant officers in Washington, D.C. My wannabe-Greer-Garson-in-*Madam-Curie* research days were done.

Sometime in May, I sold my house in Tucson. With the modest profit, I moved back into my parents' home in Nogales and spent the next several months teaching an English class at the local community center. Every now and then, when money would start to run low, my mom would throw one of her translation projects my way and I would find myself sitting at Doña Pilar's Café working on manuscript-length documents like she had always done when I was just a nosy kid tagging along with her to survey the comings and goings at the café. Most days, Lalo would sit next to me, working on his own writings. A few tables away, an almost eighty-year-old Frank Felix, by then a retired pawnbroker/loan shark, sat at his same table on the north side of the café by the big window. He still sat hunched over his coffee mug, persistently stirring nearly gone coffee yet the harmonizing "ta-ling, ta-ling" of his sidekick's spoon was missing. George Konstantinou, the petite Nogales fixture with cotton-ball hair and excessively bushy eyebrows, had passed away almost six years back.

On Thursdays, a new generation of unnecessarily loud women with flashy jewelry sat at three joined tables in the center of the café. There were at least eight or nine of them, although attendance varied depending on who had clashed with whom the previous week. Word brawls and bitchy disputes were a core element of the weekly soccer-mom gatherings that had become known across Nogales simply as *"cafés."* Although they were initially meant to be almost sacred rituals of conviviality for the women, an opportune escape from the tedious chores of their daily lives, in fact they had become just one more venue for them to try and outdo each other. It was the classic concept of one-upmanship that thrived across Nogales. When somebody brought in home-baked cookies one week, someone else would bring in a three-layered home-battered cake the following week. If someone talked about their child's gifted abilities in dance class one Thursday, a discussion of another child's extraordinary talents on the soccer field would most certainly reign the following Thursday. It was a never-ending vicious yet deeply revered cycle. For my own health, and to avoid ending up with a gratuitous headache, I studied them but only in small doses.

It was on a Thursday, as I sat at a table in the back of the café working on the Spanish version of a self-help book for co-dependent people, that I looked up to find Sasha walking into Doña Pilar's. It had been almost fourteen months since I had heard her indiscernible message on my answering machine, fifteen months since I had last seen her. She looked much thinner than I remembered her, much more fragile. The entire group of overly accessorized women at the center tables turned around to look at her. Their facial expressions were typical of all facial expressions for women who shared the same breathing space with Sasha. There was a hint of condescendence and haughtiness, but the envy and their inability to look away from her were the most evident. I too meant to look away quickly, but my neck muscles did not respond accordingly and it was only a matter of seconds before my eyes made contact with Sasha's. For a minute, I considered packing up my paperwork, getting up and leaving. Before I could finish shuffling together all my papers, though, I felt Lalo's hand on my left forearm. My face must have been a vivid picture of apprehension because he had the most gentle and calm expression, as if he was consciously trying to balance out my anxiety.

"Just listen to her, Nena." His voice was just as soothing. "You don't have to say a single word if you don't want to."

I sat still in my chair, barely breathing as I saw out of the corner of my eye as Sasha made her way slowly toward our table. When she finally reached it, Lalo stood up, greeted her with a brief kiss on the cheek and then pulled out the chair directly in front of me for her to sit. She sat down without saying a word. I looked down at the mess of papers in front of me but was not able to focus on anything other than Sasha's presence across the table from me. We sat in silence for what seemed like an eternity while Lalo walked over to the counter where Beatriz poured him two fresh mugs of coffee. When he made it back to the table, he set down the steaming mugs, closed his brown leather journal, put it under his arm and then excused himself. As I continued pretending to be absorbed by the symptoms of co-dependence described on the papers in front of me (perfectionism, excessive caretaking, hypervigilance, etc.), I saw out of the corner of my eye again as Lalo made his way out of the café. It was at that point that it hit me. Lalo had been the catalyst for our meeting.

Damn him! He had flawlessly managed to pull off one of my own tricks. After a few more awkward seconds, I finally looked up to find Sasha looking directly back at me.

"What are you doing here?" I was the first one to speak and my voice seemed to manifest a layer of harshness that even I found repulsive. Sasha shrank a bit further in her chair.

"I needed to see you, Nena." I could tell that she was trying hard to keep her voice from shaking. It wasn't working. "I've been meaning to see you for a long time, to explain things."

"Yeah, just like you've been meaning to see and explain things to Nico and Inez for over ten years now." The sardonic tones were now governing my voice. "Always trying to come off as though there's some big secret that'll eventually explain why you've been such a terrible mother and daughter and now friend." I heard the words pour out of my mouth and could barely believe that they were really coming out of me. I never knew that there could be so much anger and bitterness inside me. Big tears started to roll down Sasha's face, but the resentment inside me burned so great that it would not give way to my usual empathy or compassion.

"I'm not trying to make excuses for myself, Nena." She took a deep breath but was not able to keep from choking up. Her words were slow but audible enough between sobs. "I know how terrible a lot of things that I've done in my life have been. I've lied to a lot of people who did not deserve to be lied to. But I've also been lying to myself. I've spent years trying to fool myself into believing that I'm okay and that all the shitty things that people have done to me over the years haven't taken a toll. But it's not true. Because if you could look inside me you'd find a soul that's been shattered and broken so many times that I just don't know how to fix it anymore." She took another deep breath, that time finding the strength that she had been looking for previously. "And I've never had an army of people who come to my rescue every time that my spirit gets trampled on. People who really, truly care." She took one last deep breath. "All I ever had was you."

I continued looking at her, but after the initial outpour of words, I suddenly found myself empty. There was nothing more I could say. The empathy and the compassion were still not in me, but neither was the rage. As I sat there looking blank and emotionless, Sasha wiped the tears from under her eyes and stood up again. Her expression appeared a bit more settled.

"I'm not perfect, Nena. I've never tried to be. But in all my imperfection, I've never betrayed you and I've never lied to you." She took a few steps back, turned around and, without looking back again, walked out of Doña Pilar's Café. The powerful scent rising from the untouched coffee mugs on the table was the only thing left filling the empty space between us.

22

I didn't see Lalo for at least five days after Sasha and I exchanged words at the café. Although he showed up at my parents' house the following morning as usual, thermos and journal in hand, I did not receive him. I needed a few days all to myself. As I sat in the Arizona room looking out at the backside of Nogales, I kept going over the last words that Sasha had told me.

After the news of Alex and Sasha had died down a bit the previous year, Alex had made his first public appearance. Before a room full of reporters and high-level state politicians, he had addressed the extramarital affair issue, calling it completely fabricated and false and simply an absurd campaign to smear his and his wife's family's good name. The culprit, he had assured, had been none other than Sasha Valencia, a woman whom he had only known circumstantially in his home town of Nogales, one who clearly had a questionable and disreputable past to begin with. As he stood behind the podium addressing reporters, his wife, Emma Matthews, had been standing next to him, her face stoic and completely detached, as though it was only her shell standing next to her husband, everything else about her gutted and gone.

After the press conference, Alex appeared to go back to his regular, privileged life and the news reports and communications making references to the affair came to an almost immediate halt. I personally never called Sasha to question her about Alex's declarations, nor did she call me to explain things. The little bit of news regarding Sasha that reached me over the course of fourteen months came either through the sensationalist TV news program *Primer Impacto* on *Univision* or, after the perverse public interest in her died down, from Inez who typically only breezed through any topics related to Sasha (how she had been let go from *Jubilee!* at Bally's and was now working in a nursing home several miles away from the Las Vegas strip, for example). In reality I didn't see the point in having to confirm or validate something that was no longer relevant to me. Alex had not been a part of my life for over seven years now. He had his family and his life far away from anything that seemed even remotely familiar to me. And with Sasha, I had come to accept the fact that our lives had also reached a junction, that after so many years the time had finally come for each of us to take our separate paths. In my own way, I had already come to terms with that thought so when Sasha appeared out of nowhere at Doña Pilar's Café, my halfway settled life had been thrown into complete flux all over again.

On Saturday, Nico stopped by to visit me. Since I had been back in Nogales we had seen each other only a few times. He was fourteen years old and, given the inherent emotional strangeness that came along with adolescence, in addition to everything else that had taken place between his mother and me, I could tell that he found it difficult to talk and relate to me. When

I did see him, I always tried to make him feel at ease and complimented him on how much he was looking like his mother and how much his genuine smile reminded me of Sasha's. Most times he would just smile and look away shyly, the inner child in him gleaming. On that Saturday, though, he looked much more serious, much more mature. His light-caramel skin was just as impeccable as Sasha's had always been. Even through adolescence, I had never seen a single pimple on Sasha's face. It was as if somehow she had managed to defy the unforgiving hormonal effects that led to acne and Nico seemed to be doing the same. His yellowish-brown eyes also had a more grown-up feel to them that Monday as he sat in the wooden rocking chair across from me. I could tell that there was something important that he wanted to tell me, but it took him a few minutes before he could even look up at me. When he finally did, the words poured right out of his mouth.

"Nena, do you hate my mom now, too?"

I looked at him as he tried finding the balance between the vulnerable child that in many ways he still was and the determined, strong-minded young man that he was developing into. As he struggled to keep his emotions in check, I saw as his Adam's apple moved ever so slightly up and down in his throat and an overwhelming feeling of tenderness filled my chest. "Of course not, sweetie." I reached across and placed my hand softly on his right forearm. I could feel the muscles in his arm shaking, as well.

"Then why don't you see her or talk to her anymore?" His voice broke down a bit at the end of his last few words.

"Well… it's complicated, Nico." I really didn't know how to respond.

"What can be more complicated than having a mother that you don't even really know until you're a teenager and still being able to forgive her and love her." His voice had broken down completely at that point. My heart clenched up into a tight knot. "I've only really talked to her and gotten to know her over the past year, Nena, but it's enough to know the kind of person she is. No matter what everyone else is saying, I know my mother is a good person and I know she would never do anything to hurt anyone on purpose, especially not someone that she loves. And I know that she loves you, Nena."

I saw the tears rolling down his face and couldn't suppress the tears in my own eyes. After the failed encounter at Doña Pilar's Café more than a year ago, I had not known that Sasha and Nico had been in contact again. How come Sasha hadn't brought it up when I had accused her of being a bad mother on Thursday? Why hadn't she defended herself? I looked at Nico and could tell that he could see the confusion in my face.

"There are things that you don't know, Nena." His tone was a bit more assertive but still gentle. "If only you knew them, then maybe you'd understand."

"What things, Nico?"

"Things about where I come from and why my mom had to leave Nogales."

"Why?"

"She never wanted to leave me and she never wanted you to hurt, either."

"What are you talking about, Nico?" It was my nerves that were starting to fall apart now.

"He tried paying her off, Nena, and she didn't accept. Not that time."

"Who?"

"The man who fathered me."

"Who, Nico?" My heart felt like it was about to burst.

"Alex."

It was a week before school ended in May 1989 when Ramona walked out of the Tecolote Bar close to nine o'clock at night. She had been working the night shift for a month already. She walked out with two of the dancers and noticed a group of teenage boys walking by wearing their baseball uniforms. Late-night practices had already started for the season. Ramona heard the guys start to whistle and hurl the traditional and completely uninspired *"mamacitas,"* which all Hispanic men (both young and old) hollered out whenever they saw a female creature on the street (regardless of whether that creature was truly worthy of the compliment or not). When she turned around, she noticed both Alex and Lalo were in the bunch.

Ramona took the shortcut toward Terrace Avenue. She was still living in one of the small apartments behind Doña Pilar's Café so she went behind the bar, down the church stairway and then cut across the high school lawn. When she turned the corner to the right, past the school corridor, she heard footsteps scurrying quickly behind her. When she turned around, she noticed Alex had caught up to her. Lalo walked several steps behind them.

"Where are you heading, Ramona?" Alex's voice was as casual as always.

"Home."

"Why so early? The night's still young?" Alex joked.

"I'm tired, Alex. I've been standing for eight hours straight."

Alex turned back to look at Lalo. He seemed a bit annoyed to find him still walking behind them. "Hey, Lalo! Run home and tell mom and dad I'll be there a little bit later!"

"Where are you going?" Lalo hollered back.

"That's none of your business, just tell 'em I'll be there in a bit!"

Ramona turned to look at Alex and noticed he was serious. "Where are you really going, Alex?"

"Don't worry about it." His classic smile took a hold of his face. "I'm just gonna walk you home. There are a lot of crazy people out there, you know?"

Ramona turned back to find Lalo making his way across the street toward Elm, the street that led toward our neighborhood. She sped up her pace a bit, feeling awkward about being out so late with Alex and no one else around. She had noticed the way Alex sometimes looked at her at Doña Pilar's Café when I wasn't looking and being alone with him made her feel uncomfortable. When she saw the dim, yellow light outside of Doña Pilar's Café, she sped up even further and then turned back to tell Alex that she would be taking it from there. Alex, however, wouldn't have it.

"Are you kidding? After walking you all the way over here, you can at least offer me a glass of water, can't you? Unless, of course, you'd rather fix me one of your killer drinks." He leaned in slightly to bump his shoulder playfully against Ramona's.

Ramona didn't respond. She opened the door into her apartment and went straight into the small kitchenette, poured a glass of water from the faucet and took it back to Alex, who had made himself comfortable on the sofa bed.

"Have a seat." He patted the cushion next to him.

"No, Alex. I'm tired and I want to go to bed so you really have to leave now."

"Okay, we can go to bed if you want to then." He smiled widely at Ramona again.

"Alex, I don't think this is funny. And I don't think Nena will think this is funny, either."

Alex's face suddenly turned a shade more serious. "Don't get all defensive, Ramona. I was just joking around." He got up and handed the glass of water back to Ramona. "Listen, I was really only joking. I'm sorry if I freaked you out." His facial expression was much softer then. It was more like the Alex that Ramona was used to seeing.

"Don't worry about it." Ramona took the glass from his hand. "I'm sorry, Alex. I've just really had a long day."

Alex put his hand into his pocket and pulled out a small, perfectly round, aspirin-like white pill. "Here." He handed it to Ramona. "The coach gave it to me for my sore hamstring. If your feet or back or anything else is hurting, this'll take care of it. You'll sleep like a baby." He turned around and made his way toward the door. Before walking out he turned back to Ramona once again. "Here, I'm locking the door for you." He turned the switch on the doorknob to the locked position. "There really are a lot of crazy people out there."

Ramona watched through the small window next to the door as Alex made his way back, past Doña Pilar's toward Elm Street. She turned the front porch light off, popped the small pill into her mouth, drank the water that Alex had left in the glass and sat down on the sofa bed. Within ten minutes she felt an overwhelming heaviness take over her. She could barely even move. In a semi-alert state, she vaguely remembered cuddling up on the right side of the sofa bed and then she lost track of herself. At some point she fell asleep. When she did, she had no idea that Alex would be back, her keys in his hands. She also did not know that when she would wake up fourteen hours later, she would be pregnant with his child.

What Alex did not know when he left Ramona's apartment close to eleven o'clock that night was that, despite his careful planning and meticulousness, someone had been watching him. From behind Doña Pilar's Café, *Slugger29* had seen as his older brother came and went from Ramona's apartment a second time.

23

On Tuesday morning, the day after Nico came to visit me, I got up at seven o'clock. By 7:30, I was already filling a thermos at Doña Pilar's with enough Vienna roast for two people. When Lalo stepped out of his parents' house at 7:45 a.m., I was already sitting on the small bench by their front porch.

"Good morning." My voice coming from the left side of the porch clearly startled him. When he turned around to look at me, he seemed pleasantly surprised.

"Hey." He walked over toward the bench and sat next to me. "You brought me coffee?"

I smiled and handed him the thermos. "I forgot the cups, though. We're gonna have to steal them from your mom."

He chuckled softly, got up and brought back two mismatched coffee mugs from Marcela's kitchen. He poured the luscious brown liquid into each of the mugs and then set down the thermos on the floor to his right. We took a few sips and sat together in a comfortable silence for a good while. After a few more minutes of savoring the natural, caramelized sweetness of the coffee, I finally looked over at him.

"You never told me Alex had sexually assaulted Ramona."

He turned to look at me, his expression serious but soft. "She wouldn't let me. She made me promise I wouldn't tell anyone."

"Why?"

"At first, I guess, she was embarrassed. She felt like it was her fault, like she had maybe led him on without meaning to. And she knew that if she said anything, if it was her word against his, that no one would believe her."

"And what about afterward? When Alex came back? When he was elected mayor? When he was called up to Phoenix? She could have said something then."

Lalo shifted his whole body around on the bench until he was facing me directly. "You and Alex were very close at the time, Nena. She would have never hurt you like that."

I felt a pain of remorse pierce through me.

"Besides," Lalo continued, "she had already lived through all of the drama with Prudencio. She didn't want to expose Nico and Inez to another public spectacle."

"So Alex just got away with it?"

"When he saw the kind of political opportunities that were opening up for him, he made an agreement with Ramona. If she left Arizona and stayed quiet about everything, he would make sure that Inez and Nico were taken care of financially. That's when Ramona left for Las Vegas. She hadn't had any contact with Inez or Nico since Inez had kicked her out so she packed up her stuff and left."

"So what happened in Las Vegas last year?"

"Alex found out that he was being appointed secretary of state right around the same time that Ramona started looking for Nico again. He figured that if she made her peace with Nico and Inez that eventually she would bring up all the stuff from the past. So he got desperate and went looking for her."

"That's when those pictures were taken?"

Lalo nodded. "And it was also when he went to see you in Tucson. Ramona was avoiding him. She didn't want him to make another one of his monetary offers again. So, he thought that you might convince her to talk to him."

"But he never said anything." Images from that night at my house started to play through my mind. All I could remember was a drunken Alex babbling senselessly as he cuddled Mimi on my couch.

"He couldn't figure out how to tell you. He never found the courage to tell you the truth so he just trampled all over Ramona again. His people made up the story about Ramona trying to extort and discredit him and he just went along with it." Lalo put his left arm gently around my back. "Talk to Ramona, Nena. Whatever happened on Thursday, she knows you were in a place of confusion and pain. It's very easy for us to unload our worst sides, our most vicious words with the people we know will love us unconditionally no matter what. Forget what you said to her. She's back at Inez's. Go and talk to her."

24

Doña Pilar passed away on Thursday, December 8, 2005, one year and seven months after Ramona and I had reconciled. She was seventy years old and, consistent with everything else in her life, she died peacefully in her sleep. Despite the inevitable turns and drama that had formed part of her life over the course of seventy years, it was her characteristic serenity that made itself present on her face when she took her last breath that Thursday night.

Like her mother, Beatriz learned early on the importance of being practical and not feeding into the oftentimes unnecessary theatrics of tradition so on Friday night she arranged a small ceremony at their home behind the café. She ordered in dozens of Mexican pastries, including *conchas, cortadillos, cochitos, picones* and *elotes*, and then set up a large coffee percolator at each end of the pastries table. Although Beatriz knew that more than a few people would stop by to pay their respects to her mother, she never imagined the size of the crowd that would actually turn out. By 7:30 at night, the small house was so packed that Beatriz had to open the connecting door that led into the café and let people gather in there.

I sat next to Beatriz almost the entire night. Lalo sat to my left and sitting behind us were Inez, Nico, Ramona, Marcela, David, Fernando, Elena, Isela and my parents. At some point, I even saw Doña Lupita stop by. She walked in inconspicuously but eventually made her way over to Beatriz. As she recited yet one more biblical verse to express her condolences, a large *concha* crumb dangling from a wrinkle on the left side of her mouth, I couldn't help but feel sorry for her. She looked tired and worn out. Most heartbreaking of all, however, she looked lonely. After years of manipulating and stage-managing her daughters' lives, she had finally pushed them over the edge and each and every one of her three daughters had opted to move as far away from her as possible. As she walked past me to leave, she turned around and let an ever-so-brief smile form on her lips. It was a subtle but sincere smile. I smiled back and gently nodded a farewell before watching her slowly make her way through the crowd and back out through the front door of the house.

Close to nine o'clock, a large, black rental car pulled up in front of the café. From the driver's seat, a tall and slim chauffer wearing a traditional black suit and cap stepped out of the car. After fixing the buttons on his coat, the chauffer walked toward the rear door and opened it. From inside the car, a petite, old man with a crown of white hair and a dark overcoat slowly made his way out. It was James Mitchell, Beatriz's father.

He walked in through the café, his pace a bit clumsy and fragile. When he reached the connecting entrance into the house, he looked inside to find Beatriz already looking over at him. It took her no more than a split second to know that it was him. Despite his pale skin, his grayish-blue eyes and his white, thinning hair, Beatriz could easily see herself in her father's features. He had the same high cheekbones and the same feline-shaped eyes. For the first time since her mother's passing, Beatriz was not able to control the emotion filling her chest and the tears overflowing her hazel-brown eyes. As she got up and walked over to him, big, round tears rolled down her smooth, light-mocha complexion. After fifty years, she was meeting her father for the first time. Although they had exchanged a handful of letters and phone calls over the years, it wasn't until that night (the same night that Beatriz bid her mother a last farewell), that her father made his grand debut into her life.

I stayed at Doña Pilar's until just past eleven o'clock at night. Almost everyone else had already left. Beatriz was still sitting by her father's side in the small living room where Doña Pilar's ashes had been placed. Inez, Nico and Ramona had left at around 10:30, and Lalo's family and my family had left shortly before them. Lalo and I were cleaning the last of the serving trays when the front door to the café swung open again. Looking tired and disheveled, Alex walked in.

"Hello," he said looking a bit disoriented first over at me, then at Lalo and then back at me.

"Hi." My voice sounded tired. Lalo didn't bother responding.

"I know it's late," Alex continued. "Do you think it's all right if I step inside for only a minute?" He gestured to the doorway that led past the roasting room toward the entrance into the house. Lalo continued to ignore him. He turned around and started putting away the clean coffee mugs in the cupboard above the rear counter. I simply shrugged and lifted my left hand up slightly to direct Alex through the door. As he walked past me, I could feel his eyes trying to connect with mine again, but I intentionally looked over at Lalo instead.

It wasn't quite five full minutes when Alex walked back out from the house into the café. Lalo and I had just finished putting away the pastry dishes. He walked past the front counter slowly as if making his way toward the front door. Halfway through the table area, though, he stopped. He took a deep breath and, holding a tight grip on the black overcoat that he had been wearing on his way in, he turned around to face us again. That time he looked directly at Lalo.

"Do you mind if I have a word with Nena?" His voice had an authoritative tone to it all of a sudden. His expression had also hardened. "Alone," he added.

Lalo looked back at him matter-of-factly and then turned around to look at me. For the first time, I noticed how comforting Lalo's presence had become for me. For almost two years, during the time that Ramona and I had been distanced, Lalo had been the one constant in my life and, at that very moment as he looked gently back at me, I realized just how much his olive-green eyes had become an amulet of tranquility for me. I felt surprisingly safe around him. For the first time with anyone other than my immediate family, I felt like it was okay to be the vulnerable one, like being the protector and the one in control didn't always have to be my role. I noticed a subtle smile form on his lips and a soothing warmth filled my belly. He placed his right hand softly on my left cheek and the warmth multiplied by fifty. Before walking out of the café he leaned in and whispered, "I'll be outside if you need anything."

I watched him as he put on his dark blue jacket and casually made his way out through the front door of the café. The bright light of the desert moon delineated his slender silhouette against the soft darkness of night. When I turned around to look at Alex, he was studying me intently and he looked a bit disgruntled and annoyed. It was the same expression that I remembered of him all those years back when his lips would curl into an unpleasant smirk every time that I offered my political or intellectual view on something. He stared at me a while longer before finally speaking again.

"I see you and Lalo are getting along quite well these days."

"Yes, we are." I didn't see the need to go into a deeper explanation, especially since I knew that Alex was expecting it.

"Right." He took a few steps forward until he was standing directly in front of me on the opposite side of the counter. I could see that he was making a conscious effort to soften his facial expression as he sat down on the stool in front of me, that he was trying hard to summon back his fleeting charisma. "This place brings back a lot of good memories for me."

"Yeah, it does for a lot of people." I knew exactly where he was going.

"It reminds me of our time together. It reminds me of you, Nena." He was so predictable. I couldn't help looking unamused. I had always known that Alex was not the most original or the most creative, but his lack of creativity at that precise moment seemed much more irritating to me than usual. "Don't you ever miss us, Nena?" His voice was starting to show a hint of desperation.

I thought about my response for a long time. I didn't want to sound rash or be unnecessarily rude. I had genuinely cared for Alex for a very long time. He had been the one to awaken many unknown feelings in me for the first time and, as a matter of fact, I *had* missed "us" for many years. But as I saw him sitting there that night, I couldn't make the connection between the Alex that I had fallen for when I was a girl and the depleted, washed-out man that sat crouched on the stool before me. Despite the expensive suit and shoes, he looked withered and empty.

I must have stood in silence behind the counter where Doña Pilar had always sat longer than I realized because Alex's voice was almost frenetic when he caught my attention again. "Nena!" he said. "Are you even listening to me?"

I looked down at him and realized that my eyes had, at some point, subconsciously wandered back to Lalo as he stood by his beat-up Chevy S10 near the front window. His hair, which had been slightly fixed back for Doña Pilar's ceremony, was a mess again as he instinctively ran his fingers through it, his right hand scribbling something quickly onto yet another one of his leather journals. When he turned around briefly to look at me, an involuntary smile had formed on my lips and that had made Alex nearly flip out.

"Listen, I just thought that maybe we could talk things out." Alex's voice was uncharacteristically loud at that point, an unmanly shrill slightly perceptible. "But I see you're much too distracted."

I looked back at him and noticed how unbecoming his blue eyes were when he was irate. His skin also became red and blotchy and, most unflattering of all, his breath became short and irregular, like a spoiled kid after throwing a senseless tantrum. I considered keeping quiet as usual, just letting him vent and unload without intervening or putting in my two cents. But then he opened his mouth again.

"You two are perfect for each other, you know?" His small eyes were like pinpricks on his face as he continued. "A pair of hippies trying to change the world through their meaningless art and social work. I'm sure you'll both reach very high places." He got up from his stool and grabbed his overcoat from the counter. "Go ahead, Nena, keep your poor-man's Alex. That's all Lalo has ever been."

It was at that point that I felt the snap inside me. It was loud and forceful but completely painless. Standing in Doña Pilar's spot behind the counter, her energies channeling directly through me, I looked at Alex with a profound serenity. In the deepest corners of my soul, long-simmering thoughts and feelings were set in motion. As they rose up slowly from the core in my belly, up past my chest, a flavorful brew of words began to pour out of my mouth.

"The thing is you're a hybrid, Alex. A *caturra*. A *catimor*." I could see the confusion in his face. "Despite your apparent popularity, you tend to be bland, even mediocre in the cup." The red blotches started to take form on his face and neck again. "Lalo, on the other hand, he's a *bourbon*, a *typica*, a true heirloom variety." I looked through the front window to find Lalo still standing next to his ramshackle Chevy looking back at me, the stubborn smile forming on my lips again. "I'll take his superior and distinctive taste any day."

Alex looked at me looking at Lalo and didn't say another word. He turned around, threw on his overcoat and huffed his way out through the front door. Before making his way into his black Cadillac Escalade, he turned to look at Lalo one last time.

"You can have her," he hollered back at Lalo, who was making his way back into the café.

Lalo looked back at him, his demeanor as calm and collected as ever. "She's not yours to give, Alex. She never has been."

25

Ritual often chooses for its vehicle consciousness-altering substances such as coffee. People may assume a bit of God resides in this substance because through using it they are separated for a moment from the ordinariness of things and can seize their reality more clearly. This is why a ritual is not only a gesture of hospitality and reassurance but a celebration of a break in routine, a moment when the human drive for survival lets up and people can simply be together. This last aspect is the fundamental meaning of the coffee break, the coffee klatsch, and the after-dinner coffee. These are secular rituals that, in unobtrusive but essential ways, help maintain humanness in ourselves and with one another. – Kenneth Davids

Doña Pilar always said that coffee beans were like people, that they had to be properly cultivated if they were to be any good. And she was right. We are all shaped and sculpted by a series of factors and circumstances that ultimately determine who we will become and what our unique strengths and flavors will be.

Fertilization comes first. It is the planting of the seed that requires fertile, oftentimes volcanic, soil. In this regard, it is our mothers who, like the earth, nurture us in their wombs, diffusing their resources, their water and their nutrients to nourish us, making us healthy and strong. It is their inherent nature, before anything else, that determines what our organic composition and our inner cores will be like.

Family comes next. Regardless of its constitution or makeup, its unique shape or form, it is family who tend to us and provide the warm and frost-free climate, the sunshine but also the regular rainfall and cloud cover that are required for growing good coffee. Then, when harvest time comes around, it is the contribution of their many laboring hands (family, friends and even strangers) who patiently watch over us, waiting as we mature into the ripened fruit that must then be picked and handled with the greatest of care.

Processing or fermentation is the next step and it is perhaps the most sensitive of all stages. It is during this phase that the seeds must be freed from the surrounding protecting layers of the cherry. It is at this stage that we get to the heart of the fruit, that the care taken and the values instilled by family and friends during cultivation begin to take center stage. It is at this point that we begin to see the unique traits of the bean, its size, its color, its distinctive qualities and its individuality as it embarks on its bigger journey through life. If processing is not done correctly, if contributing hands have not been precise or careful, the path from ripe to rotten can be very short and it is never long before the coffee bean is ruined.

Roasting and grinding are the next steps and, in the bigger scheme of our lives, they represent the inevitable yet necessary trying times, those moments that sculpt and enhance the flavors locked inside each and every one of us. They are the heartbreaks and the betrayals, the misfortunes and the infidelities, the painfully excruciating episodes that, when endured with dignity and courage, help us obtain a truer sense of our inner strength, our resiliency and our integrity. They are the defining moments that force crucial changes inside us and ultimately push us to our highest flavor potential.

The last step, but by no means less important, is brewing. It is an almost artistic process that requires the simmering of just the right amount of properly roasted and ground beans with the right amount of water to extract characteristic flavors developed in the coffee bean over time. At its best, it is the harmonious and balanced union of everything (from coffee pedigree and type, to cultivation practices, to degree of roast, to bean freshness and grind) in order to produce a superlative drink experience unmatched by many. In our lives, it is that determining moment when each of our individual parts (our histories, our beliefs and values, our thoughts and emotions, our imperfections and strengths) fuse together to yield an unequivocally whole and intensely flavorful existence. The age-old question is: Is the final taste worth the wait?

Beatriz continued forth with Doña Pilar's Café, the same humble yet worldly coffee shop in the corner of Terrace Avenue and Elm Street where an entire community had gathered for fifty years to talk and gossip, read and write, think and dream. Two months after her mother's memorial ceremony, she received a letter from Tapachula, Chiapas, in Mexico notifying her that James Mitchell, her father, had also passed away. Along with the letter was a notarized legal statement informing her that she had inherited his shares in La Moka, the coffee plantation that had seen both her and her mother take their first breaths. With her newly acquired earnings, Beatriz renovated a few structural issues that were in serious need of repair around the café. For the first time, she also put up a "Doña Pilar's Café" sign that was strategically placed just above the original bright-blue, hand-painted, slightly slanted block letters -- "CAFÉ CON LECHE" -- on the top-left side of the building. She used the bulk of her new income, however, to fund a series of local community programs.

The first was a reading and writing program for bilingual children. It took place every afternoon at the café and saw as many as twenty-five children stop by to listen and write the most fantabulous stories after school. On Tuesday and Thursday evenings, a second program took place. That one was geared toward people with speech impediments and illiterate adults. Naturally, Lalo and I were thrilled to run and coordinate both programs.

On Friday nights, a third program took place. That one was more of an open mike for aspiring poets and writers. People from all over town and even a few from Nogales, Sonora, Tucson and Phoenix came by to read their poetry, or halfway finished novels, or ramblings on paper while the rest of us listened and enjoyed Doña Pilar's unforgettable coffee recipes, courtesy of

Beatriz and Ramona, who had taken over Doña Pilar's job at the café. Most nights there were as many as twenty writers, each allotted a five- to seven-minute time slot in front of the microphone. Every now and then Lalo or David would get up to read short snippets from their latest novels and the café would crowd up until people were standing outside the door by the sidewalk.

One Friday night, Nico made his debut, as well. His poem, *Morena de Fuego*, was a tribute to his mother. As I saw him standing at the microphone, his eyes looking over at Ramona as he read his rhythmically measured verses, his uncle Lalo, grandfather David and grandmothers Marcela and Inez looking on from the crowd, I couldn't keep the emotion from lodging itself in my throat and my eyes from brimming with pride and joy. It was at that moment, as I looked around the café to find my family and closest friends all around me, that I knew that the flavor in my life and the final taste of my existence had most definitely been worth the wait. Despite the bad combinations and the terribly askew blends that had only dulled and muted my flavors in the past, as I sat breathing in the smell of freshly ground and brewed coffee in the air, feeling Lalo's gentle hand softly holding onto mine, I knew that the consistency and complexity of flavor in my life was complete. It was smooth, balanced and exquisitely sweet.